I'm Open to Anything

I'm
Open to
Anything

William E. Jones

We Heard You Like Books • Los Angeles, California

PUBLISHED BY WE HEARD YOU LIKE BOOKS
A Division of U2603 LLC
5419 Hollywood Blvd, Ste C-231 Los Angeles CA 90027

http://weheardyoulikebooks.com/

Distributed by SCB Distributors

ISBN: 978-09964218-9-8

Cover photograph: *Villa Iolas (St. Sebastian by Takis)*
by William E. Jones, courtesy of the artist,
David Kordansky Gallery, and The Modern Institute,
with thanks to the Takis Foundation.

Typesetting by Iphgenia Baal

April 2021

Second Edition

9 8 7 6 5 4 3 2 1

What, do you imagine I would take so much trouble and so much pleasure in writing, do you think that I would keep so persistently to my task, if I were not preparing—with a rather shaky hand—a labyrinth into which I can move my discourse, opening up underground passages, forcing it to go far from itself, finding overhangs that reduce and deform its itinerary, in which I can lose myself and appear at last to eyes I will never have to meet again.

—Michel Foucault, *The Archaeology of Knowledge*

ONE

My birthplace was not a place at all, but a void I was afraid would envelop me in nothingness if I didn't devise a plan to escape it. When I was young, I used a compass to draw a circle with a 500-mile radius around my hometown on a map of the United States. I completely obliterated the area inside the circle with India ink, and I promised myself that one day I would leave that black hole and never return. If I couldn't see any of the cities in the region, I wouldn't be tempted to move to them and renege on the promise I made to myself.

I grew up during the 1970s and early '80s in a small industrial city in the American Midwest. I will withhold the name of it so as to spare anyone in those parts embarrassment by association. Everyone in my hometown had some connection to the local factories, and it was expected that children would grow up to follow in the footsteps of their parents. This expectation turned out to be completely misguided, because the factories started laying off thousands of workers before I reached adulthood. I imagined politicians throwing up their hands and asking, "What do we *do* with all these people?" The financiers who had forced the factories to shut down never troubled themselves with this question. No concrete solutions came from elected officials, and no workers' councils spontaneously formed to seize control of the factories and crush the power of the owners. The entire fabric of industrial society had started to unravel. Many residents of the area, unable to adapt to new circumstances or unwilling to face the economic realities right in front of their eyes, persisted in a belief that industry would return to the region one day. This was a failure of imagination: they simply couldn't envision any other way to live, and the school system, which prepared them for little more than factory work, had done nothing to help them.

When asked what I wanted to do with my life (which inevitably boiled down to how I would make money), I always mentioned some artistic vocation. The reaction would usually be "are you kidding?"; "what are you going to do with *that*?"; or most pointedly, "what are you, some kind of fairy?" The last question came from those observant enough to notice that I had no interest in football, a pastime the rules of which I never learned. It was a local obsession. (The high school football stadium contained enough seats for every single resident of the city, thirty thousand of them.) To refuse to attend football games was seen as heresy.

At a time when religious prudes pressured high schools to ban "sinful" recreational activities and censor textbooks judged to be anti-Christian, I had no religion whatsoever. I never acknowledged the fundamentalist Christianity that its adherents believed would solve their problems, making them rich through some kind of celestial lottery and sparing them from the apocalypse. I found their scriptures as incomprehensible as the activities on a football field.

To my schoolmates and my teachers, I must have appeared to be an alien influence better purged for the collective good. My attitude towards them was indifferent. To me, these people hardly seemed to exist. If they managed to register on my consciousness at all, it was as a soundtrack of white noise. Where that white noise came from and what it was masking I didn't trouble myself to consider.

If I had given more thought to my social surroundings, I probably would have been able to coast through school with a minimum of effort. From the time I was young, it was obvious that I could write, which is to say I could put a coherent sentence together and make a reasoned argument. If I had chosen anodyne topics for my writing, I would have succeeded admirably in my courses, but I couldn't help myself; I was consistently attracted to things well beyond the pale of my high school curriculum.

In an advanced composition course during my junior year, we were given an assignment to write about a work of art of our choice. From what I could see, many of my classmates chose what would properly be called commercial art, album covers or photographs of stylish commodities. The more sophisticated students chose Pop Art, which was at one remove from vulgar commerce. A couple of students who were especially eager to please chose the sort of artworks that hung in government buildings—figurative, patriotic, insipid. I chose *Doctrinal Nourishment*, a print by the Belgian artist James Ensor.

Five authority figures seated atop a wall dominate the composition of *Doctrinal Nourishment*: a general, a businessman, a bishop, a nun, and in the center, a king holding a scepter. They are all baring their asses and shitting. Below them, the common people receive their masters' excretions with open mouths. I had found a reproduction of the print in an art history book at the library, and I couldn't believe my luck. I wrote with enthusiasm about this image of the masses gobbling up shit.

The day after I turned in my essay, the teacher who had assigned it told me he wanted to see me after class. I asked him why and he gave me a stern look. When I saw him alone an hour later, he gingerly picked my paper out of a pile and slid it across his desk as though he were handling hazardous waste. I laughed and asked, "Would you prefer to wear gloves?"

"Don't try to make a joke out of this, buster. You have to rewrite that assignment if you want to pass." His face was red with anger.

"What should I write about?" I asked, trying to conceal my pleasure at the reaction I had gotten from him.

"Something abstract. That way you can't turn it into an obscenity."

"I was going for political satire," I said, and I wasn't lying.

"Leave your politics at the door. I don't need any subversive elements in my class. If you want to get into a good college, do as I say."

Suddenly, I realized that this petty tyrant might have the power to foil my plans to leave town forever. I took my paper from his desk, and that night, I wrote an essay about a Jackson Pollock painting. I restrained myself from comparing its sinuous globs of white paint to ejaculated semen. I took a pragmatic position on my writing class. If I carried my defiance further, the consequences would not have been good for my future. I wasn't proud that I had compromised my principles, if one could call expressing a childish glee at bodily functions a matter of principle, but in order to achieve a long-term goal, I backed down.

∞

I knew I wanted to do something different with my life, but I had no clue what it was. I spent a lot of time in bed. I considered staring into space to be my work. One might naturally ask—and many did—what purpose this served, and how I could justify a life lived in pursuit of no material ends. I believed this state of lassitude to be productive, if only of thought. A sympathetic person, had I ever encountered one, would have ascribed my behavior to philosophical leanings, but I was as unaware as I could possibly be of the activities of professional philosophers.

Among my contemporaries, the boys who thought highly of their intellects took to carrying copies of Ayn Rand books around school, undoubtedly because of their impressive thickness. I was not so gullible as to be taken in by the claim that these potboilers were works of philosophy. Instead, I expended great effort in trying to read Ludwig Wittgenstein. I didn't understand so much as a single word or mathematical symbol. Some years later, I took solace in a statement by Gilles Deleuze regarding Wittgenstein and his followers: "Philosophy will never die, but it has its assassins."

In a pile of books about to be discarded by the public library, I discovered a copy of the fragments of Empedocles, the Pre-Socratic philosopher. These verses written at the beginning of the Western philosophical tradition had been consigned to the trash. The copy was nearly pristine; I may have been the first person to open it in decades.

Everything about the book fascinated me. Stanzas of the original Greek text alternated with English translations. I had no knowledge of the Greek, but the shape of its letters pleased me. Only a small part of a lost whole, these fragments seemed to have more in common with magic and religion than philosophy. Empedocles believed in the transmigration of souls; about his own previous lives he wrote, "I was once already boy and girl, thicket and bird, and mute fish in the waves." He believed he could become a god as the result of his learning. Although extended passages of Empedocles survived, I was most drawn to fragments so tiny that they sounded random: "man-enfolding earth"; "the cloud-collecting"; "the belly"; and my favorite, "the blood-filled liver." These phrases were the work of translator and poet William Ellery Leonard, a man who suffered from agoraphobia, the fear of social interactions outside a very limited sphere, an anxiety disorder named for the public square of ancient Athens, the Agora.

I knew that Empedocles had a young companion called Pausanias, who was his *erômenos*, a Greek word commonly translated as "beloved." I soon learned that the word also suggested that Pausanias got fucked by Empedocles. This came as a revelation to me. At that moment, I started on a new path of understanding. Supposedly neutral words could be hiding other meanings that made old Victorians uncomfortable, and therefore were passed over in silence. I began to search for the hidden meanings that lay behind common language. Some would say I had a dirty mind, but these people very likely had no need to conceal their true thoughts, because they had none to conceal.

Empedocles entrusted his young lover and disciple with secrets. He addressed the poems to Pausanias and offered him this advice, "Shelter these teachings in thine own mute breast." I considered the meaning of Empedocles' message for my own life. I learned to be careful how much I revealed about my personal habits. I believed that if I kept my head down, I might be able to avoid a fate I dreaded, whether it be as dull as the life of a factory worker, or as dramatic as the suicide of Empedocles, who purportedly killed himself by leaping into the volcanic crater of Mount Etna. I understood that my imagination contained things better kept secret. I also knew that devotion to intellectual labor for its own sake was liable to inspire resentment at a way of life perceived as wasteful. Wasteful of what, I felt compelled to ask. As far as I could see, the reality transpiring all around me was one giant waste.

∞

My parents very kindly provided me with the means to stay alive, but they had so little understanding of their son that I might as well have been a mute fish in the waves. My father was the plant manager of a factory that assembled automotive parts. My mother worked part time as a bookkeeper at a steel mill. We had become accustomed to thinking of ourselves as middle class, like most Americans of the time. My parents had an inkling that everything they expected from life was not forthcoming, and being burdened with a lay-about son added to their sense of grievance. The nearly total silence I maintained in their presence drove them to distraction. With the discipline of an ascetic, I asked for very little. I wanted freedom, not material objects. One family member who happened to see my bedroom gasped and said, "It looks like a monk's cell" in a tone that implied "there's something not right about the boy."

By way of explanation, my mother would say something about me being "sensitive," which everyone understood as a euphemism for being queer, either sexually or mentally. My relatives accepted this without question, sometimes with a downcast glance and a shake of the head. I disagreed with my mother's description of me, but I did not contradict her. She was describing the son she wanted: a sensitive mama's boy who occupied himself with doing crafts, styling her hair and makeup, and showering her with presents. The son she actually encountered in daily life mystified her. Calling someone sensitive implies deep feelings. At that time, I could locate few feelings within myself. I had surmised that the best way to get through the first years of my life was to be numb. I touched no one, nor was I touched, and I observed everything happening around me as though from a distance.

∞

My father's drinking, which had always been a problem, became much worse during my junior year of high school. He was about as taciturn as I, and at first he said nothing about what precipitated this new phase of his decline. I eventually learned the details: someone at the factory where he worked had suffered a horrific accident.

A mechanical press used to stamp metal parts had cut off all ten fingers of a young man my father was training. They had been standing right next to each other, and my father saw everything. He was able to call for help immediately and to find a cooler with ice. He placed the severed fingers in the cooler, while another worker applied pressure to stop the bleeding from what was left of the young man's hands. A doctor came from another city to perform a complex operation at the local hospital. In the end, most but not all of the young man's fingers were reattached, though their range of movement would be limited. After recovering from surgery, the patient would be able to wipe his ass, but he'd never play the piano.

The accident provoked a series of legal actions against the factory and its employee, my father. The cases hinged on whether the company had been negligent or not, if all the proper safety guards and warning signs had been in place, and whether my father had done everything he could to prevent the accident. A window of time, no more than a couple of hours, was recounted over and over. My father gave depositions, and lawyers questioned him on several occasions. Before each meeting with the lawyers, he spent the night drinking such great quantities of liquor that I wondered if he would succumb to alcohol poisoning. Perhaps my father's incapacitated state was what necessitated the numerous meetings; it certainly suggested that he had been drinking on the morning of the accident.

The status of my father's employment went through several changes over the course of those months. First he was fired, then rehired as manager on the advice of legal counsel, then finally given a sinecure, a menial position in which he could cause no harm during the period leading up to the resolution of the lawsuit. When it came to light that the young man bringing suit was a habitual pot smoker, an out of court settlement quickly followed. My father was spared the ordeal of a lengthy civil trial, which was best, because by the time the settlement was reached, he had become virtually catatonic.

In the wake of these events, the family disintegrated. My father, haunted by guilt about the accident and nurturing an obsessive hatred of lawyers, could not work. He didn't qualify for disability benefits, and he didn't have the resources for a detoxification program. My mother worked more hours at her job, and the wife of one of the executives took an interest in her. They began to socialize from time to time, and this woman introduced my mother to local politics. These activities provided a welcome escape from my father.

For others under such circumstances, nothing would have been possible, but to me, it appeared that anything was possible. The need to escape became intense, and college applications offered me a perfect opportunity. I applied only to universities outside the black circle I had drawn around my hometown. There was little to lose in uprooting myself entirely and starting a new life elsewhere. I concentrated all of my efforts on making as decisive a break with my childhood as I could.

TWO

My time in college reminded me of an aphorism often repeated by William S. Burroughs: "Some people are shits, darling." I had left a shitty town, only to be surrounded by shits on a college campus. After spending years dealing with kids who wanted to beat me up because I was a fag, I had to deal with adults whose sense of propriety restrained them from beating me up, but whose disdain for me was obvious. They insulted me not only because I was a fag, but also because I came from nowhere, and I knew little about the things they held in high esteem. Many of my conversations with classmates carried a subtext of nagging questions: "who let you in?" or "why are you here?" In being admitted to this fine university, I had been given the key to another world, but I hadn't been given instructions for how to use it.

I made few friends during my time in college. Most of the students I befriended eventually revealed themselves to be just as committed to convention and intolerance as the people of my hometown. The main differences were the level of their parents' incomes and the breadth of their horizons. I realized sooner or later that I had nothing much in common with them.

There was only one person with whom I felt comfortable. Moira was a class behind me, and she was one of the freaks on campus. Most people shunned her, but I thought her fearlessness was wonderful. In a way, she had no choice in the matter. She was almost six feet tall, with platinum blonde hair and skin so pale that it seemed almost translucent. She would have stuck out no matter what she did. She had gotten seriously involved in leftist politics, on campus and off. Her passion was opposing the United States' involvement in the ongoing carnage in Central America. She spoke fluent Spanish and wanted to use it to help the cause as soon as she graduated.

Moira's politics set her apart from the great majority of the students I knew, but there was something else, an attitude I imagined came from having grown up in Los Angeles. I got the impression that she had seen everything and done everything, despite the efforts of the girls' school she attended to keep her sheltered. Instead of turning her into a bored, dismissive sophisticate old before her time and dead on the inside—a fate awaiting many of our classmates—her experience had turned her into someone very wise and generous, at least to those not among the despised ruling class.

I lent Moira a sympathetic ear, but she never managed to convince me to join her at any meetings or marches. In unguarded moments, once she was satisfied that I didn't work for the FBI or CIA, Moira said some delightful things. She described President Reagan as a "glad-handing retard" and his wife Nancy as the "blow job queen." She denounced the Republicans' inroads among the white working class, a trend she recognized very early. Their deceptions, which convinced voters to act in conflict with their objective interests, were the chief reason (among many) that she believed in doing away with representative democracy. I asked what she proposed in its place, and she responded, "direct democracy of workers' soviets, the dictatorship of the proletariat." How this would be achieved was a subject of constant and intense speculation for her. She often spoke about the complete liquidation of the political classes of the United

States, a severe program of mass executions, many conducted inside the very houses of the Congress. I asked on what charge thousands of government officials would be convicted and condemned. She paused for a moment and said, "We'll think of something." Such radical actions might be gratifying in the short term—who wouldn't enjoy the spectacle of venal old hypocrites gutted like quivering fish?—but I suspected they would lead only to the replacement of the social class in power by another class every bit as vicious as the former oppressors, if not worse. The examples of previous revolutions offered little hope in this regard. Not wanting to be denounced as a reactionary, I kept my objections to myself as she elaborated her theories. During her unbalanced visionary moments, I felt she was the only person on campus I truly loved.

I got the impression that Moira loved me back. Neither of us put our feelings into words, because her plans for the coming revolution took priority, and because my feelings were not nearly as intense as hers. We didn't want to disturb the delicate balance between us. That balance was destroyed when one of Moira's relatives came to visit.

Although no one would guess it from looking at her, one branch of Moira's family was Hispanic. Her cousin Al (short for Alcibiades) came from Cuba. He lived in Los Angeles and attended film school. Al exuded a personal magnetism that I found overpowering. He looked like a *macho*, but he was clearly gay. He kept his hair cropped short, and he sported a bushy moustache. His powerful torso and large pectoral muscles were covered with thick black hair I could see though the white t-shirt that was his normal attire unless rain or cold weather forced him to put on a leather jacket. He always seemed to be on the verge of bursting out of his blue jeans. There was a worn spot right at the crotch. He kept the bottom button of his fly unbuttoned, and from what I could tell, he never wore underwear. On clear days, he wore athletic shoes, and on rainy days, he wore motorcycle boots.

I stared at Al whenever I got a chance, which was fairly often, since Moira and I lived in the same building. I made no attempt to hide my fascination. I inspired no interest at all. I wasn't aware of it at the time, but Al only acknowledged men who looked more or less like him. Al was a clone. This derisive term described gay men of nearly identical appearance who moved in packs in urban areas around that time. They excelled at disco dancing, sex, and gossip. Their carefully cultivated *machismo* presented itself only as an image. Often the moment they opened their mouths, the illusion was shattered.

One day I saw Al and Moira in the courtyard of our building. The two of them spoke in Spanish. He talked very quickly and in a domineering way that struck me as slightly absurd, because his hands were flying all over the place making emphatic gestures. They were so absorbed in conversation that they didn't see me watching. I approached them and noticed that Moira was in tears. I could only make out one sentence: Al said, *Él es maricón.* (He is a fag.) I knew at once that he was referring to me, and I turned and walked away.

The day after Al returned to Los Angeles, I asked Moira about her cousin. A part of me hoped she would say, "he really likes you," but she said nothing of the sort. Instead, she summarized his biography, beginning with a political preamble: "Cuba's revolution was a fundamental step in liberating oppressed peoples, and the country is a bulwark against Western capitalist imperialism right on the doorstep of the United States. But unfortunately, Cuba's revolution has become authoritarian in some respects. People perceived as counterrevolutionaries suffer. Due to traditional *machismo* and (from what I have heard) the secret homosexuality of certain leading members of the Communist Party, gay men have been treated like shit in Cuba since the beginning of the 1960s. Petty surveillance enforces conformity. Men denounced as 'extravagant' or 'anti-social'—euphemisms for 'effeminate'—end up in reeducation camps or prison. Anyone who has even an occasional desire to suck a cock lives in a state of constant anxiety and paranoia. Rooting out homosexuality has become an obsession with the party leaders, who strike many observers as a bunch of hysterical, self-hating closet cases.

"Al comes from the part of my mother's family that didn't leave Cuba in 1959 or '60. They were poor intellectuals and leftists, and they thought they would have better lives in the land of revolution. For most of them, this was undoubtedly true, but for Al, who acted like a little princess as a boy, the future looked grim.

"When Al was a teenager, a number of gay intellectuals and artists tried to find political asylum at foreign embassies, and all of them were refused. They got sent to prison. Then in 1980, the situation at the Peruvian Embassy reached a critical moment, and the ambassador was recalled to Lima. The Cuban government left the embassy grounds unguarded for a few days, and during that time, thousands of asylum seekers gathered in a space the size of a football field. Al was one of them. He had decided to leave his family behind and try to make a life for himself abroad. It was a total nightmare—no food, no water, and constant harassment for days at a time—what they call a humanitarian crisis in the news. His family was mortified. One of our cousins tried to help him by bringing food and water. She was arrested. Finally, Al got on a boat leaving the port of Mariel for Key West. It was an ordeal. I think he was raped and beaten on the way. He won't talk about it, but something awful happened.

"Al finally got to Miami and stayed with relatives from the older, bourgeois generation, and once he learned English and finished high school, they paid for him to go to film school in LA. His American family is as reactionary as you would expect, and they love their adopted country. Al himself has mixed feelings about the United States. If you don't grow up under capitalism, this country is a complete shock. You have the freedom to be gay, but everything has a price, and this mercantile aspect of life poisons every social interaction. Al's lucky that he can go to film school, but our family does *not* know what he's doing there."

"What are his films about?" I asked.

"Drag queens. And he makes a living by working in the gay porn industry."

"Wow, is he a porn star?" I tried not to sound too excited by the thought.

"No," Moira said, "He's a cinematographer. He borrows a camera from school to shoot pornos on the weekends." I thought about Al filming guys fucking. I wondered if he had had sex with porn stars. Moira, probably noticing my mind wandering, stuck to her own agenda for the conversation. "It's horrible that Cuba is so backward when it comes to the gay question, but I still believe that the standard of living for nearly everyone is better than it would have been under the dictatorship of some American puppet."

Moira seemed genuinely anguished by the contradictions of contemporary Cuba. She wanted to have unalloyed faith in a socialist state, but her cousin's experience did not encourage her. Ever the romantic, she hoped the next revolution would turn out better. I loved her adherence to principles most would have dismissed as quixotic, but it occurred to me that her anguish had a personal dimension as well. The tears I saw a few days before in the courtyard had less to do with the problems of building socialism in the Western Hemisphere than with the phrase *él es maricón*.

∞

During my last semester of college, my mother called to tell me that she and my father couldn't come to graduation. All she would say at first was, "Your father hasn't been well." This was her way of saying that his drinking was out of control.

"What now?" I asked in a weary tone.

"Something happened," my mother said, arriving at the point. "He vomited blood last week."

I was startled. "That's serious. He belongs in a hospital."

My mother started sobbing. She knew what I said was true, and she also knew that she had no way of coping with the situation in a sensible way. Once she got hold of herself, she said, "You'd better come home right after graduation."

I resented my mother calling a place I so clearly did not belong "home," but I held my tongue. I said, "I'll pack up my stuff and rent a van. See you in May."

∞

A heat wave made the experience of commencement almost unbearable. As an orphan of sorts, I skipped the family-oriented events, and there was little left to do besides attending a ceremony where I wouldn't get my actual diploma. While my classmates were celebrating, I was in my room, throwing out most of my possessions. I packed what was left in boxes. There were no vans available at the rental company, so I was forced to cram everything into a compact car.

My telephone line had not yet been turned off, and I received two calls on my last day of packing. The first was from an uncle I barely knew. He spoke with a broad accent that sounded military. He rambled on about how important it was that I had gotten my degree. I was the first person in the family to have graduated from college, and big things were expected of me. I detected a note of contempt in his congratulations. His tone implied a question: if all my other relatives did just fine with high school diplomas, what made me so special? I couldn't wait to get off the phone with him.

The second call came from Moira. She offered to come over and help me pack. I told her I was nearly finished but would like some company. A short while later, she arrived at my place with a pitcher of iced tea and a cassette tape by The Cure. "Guillermito, I'll miss you!" she said by way of greeting. The Spanish diminutive was an inside joke, the exact meaning of which I could no longer recall, something to do with a transvestite in a Mexican short story. She put on the tape, which was cued to one of our favorite songs, "All Cats Are Grey."

"You're saving my life with that tea. I'm parched." I drank a whole glass at one go and wiped my forehead.

"I've come to say so long. I'm leaving too. I'll be in Central America next semester."

"Umm… is that safe?" I asked.

"My personal safety is a trivial matter," she said with a finality that put an end to the discussion. She asked, "What about you? Where will you be in the fall?"

"No plans. I'm needed at home. My father is dying."

Moira shuddered and said, "I'm sorry."

I looked at my boxes for a moment, then I sat down on the bed next to her. "What the hell am I going to do?" I tried not to whine. "My father has been killing himself for years now. I don't want to get stuck in that place."

She hugged me and said, "You should move to California."

"But I've never been there!" I said, simultaneously shocked and pleased.

"So what? Once you're on the West Coast, you can reinvent yourself completely. Lots of people do it. And you'll probably be able to pull it off. You won't know until you try."

I said, "I guess so."

"Go west, young man," she said in a mock-portentous tone. Then she admitted, "I'm a little jealous, you know? I'm from LA, so I can't move any farther west. I guess that's one reason I'm going south. One reason." Her conversation trailed off, because she didn't want to say too much, then she continued. "Anyway, it's a place where you have license to do *anything*." She raised her eyebrows. There was another pause. She got up and grabbed a pen and paper from my desk. She wrote down a phone number and address. "Here. My parents live in Hancock Park, and I'm sure you can stay with them a couple of weeks while you find your own place. Hancock Park isn't where you want to live, but it's central. You'll probably prefer Highland Park."

I didn't know the difference between Hancock Park and Highland Park. Like a lot of people, all I knew about the city came from the movies I'd seen, which were a rather unreliable guide, to hear Moira tell it. The only recent movie that she thought captured something of Los Angeles was *Repo Man*. We had seen it together at a theater around the corner from where we lived. She told me she had her problems with the film, but secretly she was thrilled when she recognized a glimpse of the city she knew. *Repo Man* made the place look like a giant hick town full of people with terrible attitudes. The plot was ludicrous, but the shots of driving around downtown and East Los Angeles, back and forth across the bridges over the Los Angeles River, had an atmosphere I hadn't seen before in a movie. Drag racing in the bed of the river—actually, a huge concrete ditch—was strictly for the movies; no one was allowed to do that. In a bar scene, the punk band The Circle Jerks appeared as an incompetent and smarmy lounge act. When she saw them, Moira laughed, then turned to me and whispered in my ear, "They played at my high school prom." I was impressed.

I was even more impressed by Emilio Estevez, who played the main character, Otto. In the film, he's beautiful and kind of an asshole but very charming. He has the worst attitude of all, flinging a statue of the Virgin Mary out the window of a car he repossesses, asking for a blow job from his girlfriend while she's at work, stumbling into his parents' house and asking for $1000 as he eats out of a tin can. (He doesn't get the money; his parents have given it to a television preacher who says he's buying bibles for El Salvador, a line that made Moira snort in disgust.) I wondered how many guys like Otto were living in Los Angeles, and how I could meet them. It was at that moment I first entertained the idea of moving there.

At the end of her visit, I asked Moira if she had a phone number where I could reach her. She said, "No, it's better if I write to you." I thought that sounded suspicious, but I didn't press her on the issue. I never did. Moira delivered her parting words to me in an offhand way. "You should write about your experiences. I'm sure it would be interesting." I kissed her on both cheeks and she left.

∞

I arrived at my parents' house with a dozen boxes of clothes and books. Although it was only May, the weather was sweltering, and without air conditioning, the place was a sweatbox where any movement required great effort. That first evening, I lay down on my bed and didn't get up for twelve hours. All of the boxes remained in piles, packed and sealed. Even when rain came and the temperature dropped a few days later, I could barely get out of bed. I had the overwhelming feeling that I was trapped and would never make my way out of the black circle I'd drawn on the map years before.

My father's condition had improved, and he didn't say a word about his recent crisis. My mother said little more. She avoided any serious discussion and was often away from home, her excuse being a new job at the local Republican Party headquarters. While she was at work, my father sat in his chair and watched television all day. He only stirred to make trips to the state liquor store. How he could drive, and when he drove, how he avoided being stopped for drunk driving, I was never able to determine. I refused to be a passenger in his car. I would borrow it regularly, and as long as I didn't interfere with his daily errand, he didn't seem to mind.

My mother had given me the impression that my father was dying and my presence at the family home was absolutely necessary.

It seemed to me that my father was, if not well, at least in the same state of health as the last couple of years. I began to wonder if I had been tricked. I thought my parents, consciously or not, were subverting my attempt to lead an independent life after college. They wanted me to be as unhappy as they were.

To be fair, I hadn't given my parents any reason to think I would be a great success, or even moderately skilled at navigating adult life. The chief problem was my credit card debt. Inexplicably, a bank had offered me a credit card while I was in college. I used it for necessities at first, then for things that some would call frivolous, including a trip to Europe. I traveled alone, saw a lot of museums, took many trains, and was generally miserable. (It was pissing rain most of the time.) I felt no regret, but I eventually came to understand that the debt I had accumulated could not be paid off unless I found a job with a substantial salary, something I could hardly imagine doing. I decided that I would file for bankruptcy while I lived with my parents. I couldn't blame them if they thought I was a fuck-up.

I began to spend more and more time out of the house. My days would follow a set pattern. After breakfast, I would go out and return in time for lunch. I ate in front of the television, watching the news as my father left to buy vodka. The sound of the electric garage door opener signaled his return, and when I heard it, I got up and started clearing away plates and utensils. My father would usually come in as I was washing the dishes, and while my back was turned, he hid his liquor bottle in a cabinet next to his chair. (I never saw any empties, but I figured his habit by that time must have been a bottle of vodka per day.) He would get back into his chair and grumble about what was on television or how the world was going to hell until I changed the channel for him at one p. m. so he could see his favorite soap opera. I went back to my room and waited until I heard snoring. Then I would take his keys and go out again.

To justify my wanderings, I invented a project for myself. I would scout locations for a film. I explored the industrial wasteland my hometown had become and made sketches and notes. I didn't have the means to produce a film, but this didn't stop me from filling notebooks with enough material for a feature length project. After a few weeks I took an old camera I found in the basement and started shooting black and white still photographs. This activity proved to be too conspicuous, and the local residents assailed me with questions and sometimes threats. They treated me like some sort of spy or child molester. No one had come into their neighborhoods before to take pictures, and they assumed I was up to no good. I stopped taking photographs after a few rolls; I had no facilities to develop or print them anyway.

On a typical day, I would return in time for dinner, usually fast food that my mother brought home after work. Over dinner she would tell us about what had happened at headquarters, which interested me about as much as my father's soap operas. I never got the sense that my mother worked for the Republicans out of deep political conviction. She mainly did it to avoid my father and do a bit of social climbing at the same time. She spent her days gossiping with conservative biddies who were, as the newspapers put it, "socially prominent" in the area. My mother had grown up poor, so to be accepted by these fossils meant a lot to her. The party took advantage of this at every turn, putting my mother to work organizing events with donors the old guard thought were beneath them socially. I'm sure that behind my mother's back, they made fun of the trace of a southern accent she never managed to lose, and her lack of understanding of the subtle class distinctions that gave them a reason to live. They exploited her ability to be nice to everyone—something that was beyond them—and her skill with formal correspondence. The success of the Republican Party depended absolutely upon the traditional elites making alliances with people they secretly hated, like my mother. She would talk with pride about all the famous politicians she had met, but I refused to be moved by her stories. I suppose in withholding attention from her I was being as sadistic and contemptuous as those Republican gargoyles in pumps and pearls. I now think that my mother must have been incredibly lonely, but at that time, I couldn't acknowledge it. I was preoccupied with my own loneliness.

THREE

In early June, I started unpacking the boxes brought home from college. I hadn't labeled them, so I didn't know what I would see inside any given box. I was hoping to retrieve my porn collection, but I had no luck in my first attempts to find it. I wanted my favorite item: a sixty-four page full-color magazine called *Hard Fucking Buddies*. I stole it from a classmate during my sophomore year. I finally found it, and while my father snored in the living room loudly enough to be heard through walls, I jerked off.

Afterwards I looked through the back pages of the magazine, where I saw a few advertisements for paperback novels, sex toys, super-8 films, and vhs tapes. I knew nothing about any of the movies listed except what I read in the ad copy. I couldn't afford the extravagance of buying videos sight unseen at $89.95, but I saw one title, *Good Hot Stuff*, on sale at a budget price of $49.95, which was still a fortune to me. The tape was a compilation of movies produced by Hand In Hand Films, and included scenes from *Lefthanded*, *Hot Pants*, *Wanted: Billy the Kid*, and others. That evening I asked my mother for money to buy some necessities like a new pair of shoes. The next day, I got a money order for $49.95 (plus shipping and handling) and sent it with a signed statement that I was twenty-one years of age.

The tape didn't show up for weeks. The law allowed a business to hold a customer's payment for thirty days before shipping an order, and that is exactly what Hand In Hand did. Then I waited another week for the package, sent book rate, to show up at my parents' house. Since my father never bothered to go to the end of the driveway after returning from his daily errand and the mail generally arrived at two in the afternoon, there was no chance of him intercepting my package. I returned from my wanderings by five p. m. to make sure my mother wouldn't intercept it, either. I finally received *Good Hot Stuff* in mid-July.

Since the VCR and television were in the living room, and my father was constantly in his chair during the day (and often sat in it all night as well), I could only look at my new purchase at lunchtime. My father's daily vodka run generally took twenty minutes, so I could never watch *Good Hot Stuff* in its entirety, nor could I masturbate while watching, unless I did it very quickly. As soon as my father left the house, I would grab my video, put it in the VCR, and watch as much as I could until I heard the sound of the electric garage door opener. I would then press stop and eject, hoping the old top-loading VCR didn't mangle the tape, and retreat to my room.

Good Hot Stuff got off to a slow start. The film doesn't simply string together a bunch of disconnected scenes, but includes a lot of introductory and interstitial material, because the producers at Hand In Hand took themselves seriously as filmmakers. *Good Hot Stuff* shows crew members milling around a set preparing scenes, directors screening rushes and working at an editing table, and the Hand In Hand composer discussing music. The narrator, Mark Woodward, looks like an androgynous hippy, already unfashionable by the time of the film's release in 1975, and speaks with an affectation that makes him sound perpetually jaded. For some reason, many of his appearances involve getting makeup applied to his face. Up to that point, I had no idea that porn actors ever wore makeup on the job. I imagined Mark moving to San Francisco after his work in the film. There he would befriend a group of women wearing thrift store frocks and cat-eye glasses and speaking in accents sounding like an imitation of Katherine Hepburn in *Stage Door*. I didn't find this thought sexually exciting in the least. Some of the men performing in *Good Hot Stuff*'s scenes weren't bad, though. The majority of them looked to me like the sort of dirtballs who walked down any city street, but with more expensive clothes.

After several days of furtive mid-day porn watching, the tape reached a segment from *Drive*, a big budget production about "fifty very compulsive men," as the tagline put it. One scene starts with a drag queen played by Christopher Rage (who later directed his own films) saying, "Good evening, my name is Arachne. Welcome to the club."

The narrator continues, "'Welcome to the club' is right, and a featured attraction in another outstanding scene from *Drive* is a double fist fuck. It's a triple mind fuck." A shot of a hand going in and out of a hairy ass immediately follows. There is no buildup, just an action like a piston in an engine, shown in extreme close up. White grease covers the fister's hand and the fistee's ass. (Their faces are never shown.) Later in the scene, the bottom gets fisted by two men, one with nearly an entire forearm inside his ass and the other sliding a hand alongside the first man's arm. Then the top from the beginning of the scene fists two bottoms simultaneously, one with each hand. The shooting and editing create an effect so chaotic that it's difficult to tell exactly what is going on. Generous amounts of amyl nitrate must have confused everyone on set. The music, which mixes obscene heavy breathing, dissonant chords, an elephant trumpeting, and possibly a vacuum cleaner, sounds as if it had been recorded during a cocaine binge, or was intended to be the aural equivalent of one. It was so loud that I missed my normal cue, the garage door opening. As my father came through the back door, I ejected the tape without stopping it first, but fortunately, I didn't hear the crunching sound I sometimes heard when I wasn't careful. I hid the tape under a cushion of the sofa until my father passed out an hour later.

∞

The month of August brought oppressive humidity relieved only by thunderstorms. On one especially awful morning, I woke up to silence. I didn't hear my mother getting ready, my father snoring, or the television blaring. I looked at the clock by my bed: it was nearly ten a. m. I rolled over, and half asleep, wondered if I could escape the heat by going to a matinee at the local movie theater. The challenge would be finding a decent movie. My father used to take me to movies almost every week from the time I was a small child. He needed company, and what he wanted to watch rarely appealed to my mother. He always chose the film, and even if it was age-restricted, he would bring me along. I saw my first grown-up movie, *Bonnie and Clyde*, when I was about four years old. I missed those days of doing something a bit illicit with my father. I considered asking him if he wanted to join me that afternoon, though it was unlikely he'd be in any shape to make the trip.

When I noticed that it was after eleven a.m. and the house was still silent, I decided to get up and check on my father. The door to my parents' bedroom was closed but unlocked. I opened the door without knocking. A horrible smell in the room hit me. My father lay on his back, propped up slightly on a pillow, naked, as he tended to sleep in summer. All over his chin and chest there was blood so dark that it looked black in the dim light. He had shit the bed and vomited. I nearly gagged and couldn't approach him for a moment. I opened the curtains and saw that he was pale, almost gray. I called "Dad" with no response. I slapped his arm, once again with no response. His skin was cold, and I tried and failed to find a pulse at his wrist. I bolted out of the room and called an ambulance.

I unlocked the front door and dressed in a hurry. Then I stood close to my father, hoping that he would miraculously spring out of bed or at least start breathing, and waited for the ambulance to arrive. He had once been tall and thin and handsome, but decades of drinking had distorted him into a large shapeless mass. His belly was distended, but it still did not obscure his penis, which jutted out at an aggressive angle, as though he had just opened his trousers to piss. It was darker and pinker than the rest of his flesh. It looked rather flat, wider than it was thick; it would have been oblong in cross section. He had a foreskin that covered most but not all of the head, which seemed to have a drop of moisture at the tip. I had never had the opportunity to study my father's penis at length. During my childhood, I saw it a few times in public rest rooms, but its size scared me so much that I always turned away quickly. It must have been at least eight inches long and six inches in circumference as I saw it in front of me. I wondered if my father had died with a partial erection. I was about to estimate the size of his testicles when I heard a commotion at the front door.

The paramedics had arrived, but they couldn't get their gurney through the doorway. I had to open the garage door and let them in the back. I stood in the living room and watched as they struggled to get their equipment to my parents' bedroom. I realized at that moment how small the house was—the hallways were cramped, the doors narrow, the walls close. It was an inappropriate thought to have in an emergency, but that's what came to me.

I slowly made my way to the bedroom. One of the paramedics was calling someone. He hung up the phone and said, "We have to wait for the coroner." That was when I realized my father was dead.

At the morgue, I called information to get the number of Republican Party headquarters. It took three calls to reach my mother. They were preparing for a visit from George Bush, and the place was in a frenzy. I was so impatient by the time she came to the phone that I blurted out, "Dad is dead."

My mother arrived in a taxi. She wasn't able to drive. She found me in a waiting room and sat down next to me. She couldn't finish a sentence without crying. I led her to the front desk and asked what she had to do. She filled out some forms, and we took a taxi back home.

The next week passed in a daze. I couldn't believe how many things required my mother's attention: funeral arrangements, getting copies of the death certificate and presenting them at various places, finding a new mattress for the bed she had shared with my father for over twenty years. In a quiet moment, she said, "I'm glad you came home." My father had actually been close to death, and she had known it.

I helped my mother as best I could. None of the biddies from work offered any help, though they did come to the memorial. One of them had a heart attack during the service and was taken away in an ambulance. I was too distracted to feel upset that she had upstaged my father at his own funeral.

In the weeks following my father's death, it became clear that whatever family money there had ever been was long gone. Even as he died from alcoholism, my father always handled the family finances, and my mother never suspected any problems, despite her husband having been unemployed or unemployable for a number of years. She did her best to hide all of this from her social circle, but I don't see how they could have been ignorant of it. Perhaps their presence at my father's funeral had been a sort of reconnaissance mission, like their regular attendance at church, to accumulate gossip fodder. I think my mother's goal was to project an image of genteel poverty, which would have been possible if the family had been genteel to begin with. Embarrassed that my father had left me nothing after his death, she gave me his car (a big American sedan from the early 1980s with low mileage and not yet rusted out) plus a couple thousand dollars she managed to get from somewhere. She told me not to expect anything more, because it didn't exist. She asked me, "When do you think you'll start looking for work?"

I said, "Sooner or later, but it won't be here. I'm moving to California." I don't know what my mother expected me to say, but she looked completely surprised. I continued, "I want to get there by the end of September. I'll stay with the family of a friend. I'll let you know when I have my own address and phone number."

I'm sure my mother was shocked by how coldly I approached the situation, planning to abandon her at the moment she most needed support. Looking back on it, I could have been kinder or more tactful, but the truth of the matter was that for many years my fondest desire had been to get the hell out of town, and she had given me the means with which to do so. The idea that I'd use money and a car for such a purpose must have occurred to her.

"Why do you have to move so far away?" she asked with tears in her eyes. My mother had never lived more than ten miles from where she was born and had never seen anything west of Chicago. To her, California was merely an image, vague and iniquitous, about which she (like all Midwesterners) knew a single thing: it was a place from which one did not return.

"What else can I do?" I asked. "Here there's no future."

FOUR

In September, I drove across the United States. When I saw what lay beyond one hundred degrees longitude for the first time, I knew I would live in the American West for the rest of my life.

I hated Los Angeles. The horrific traffic, the relentless sunshine and blank skies, the very private and mysterious aspect of a city where nothing is obvious—I found them all frustrating, and a long time passed before I realized that these were not things to hate but practically civic virtues. The city did not give itself away to any tourist; I had to work to discover it.

During my first two weeks in California, I spent whole days driving around aimlessly, looking for a place to live and a neighborhood where I might feel at home. I passed seemingly endless rows of storefronts and industrial parks, strip malls and Spanish Revival style boxes. Although I found this experience alienating, it occurred to me that Los Angeles was the best city for a lay-about like me. There were many "for rent" signs around, the asking price for an apartment was not very high, and the landlords were not too picky about the sort of person to whom they rented. I could have my own place in this city, and no one would be snooping around or looking over my shoulder.

Los Angeles has a lamentable lack of public spaces, and feeling at ease outside a private room sometimes seems impossible. It is as though the entire urban landscape reverberates with a dismal message: "You are lost; the place you seek does not exist." For a social butterfly or a run of the mill exhibitionist who needs the attention of others to feel complete, Los Angeles is hell on earth. For someone who feels more comfortable alone, it is perfect. In this place one can refine new extremes of individualism and perversion, as long as there is space to experiment.

I gravitated towards Silverlake, which had a rundown, bohemian air. There were bookstores and coffee houses, and a guidebook I found listed many gay bars in the neighborhood. The grid of Los Angeles changes its angle there, and in the hills, the pattern of streets becomes a maze. I got lost more than once. Along Hyperion Avenue, there was a cluster of bars interspersed with auto shops and other small businesses. I later found out that a few of those nondescript buildings were sex clubs.

Near the end of one of my drives, I found myself at the corner of Sunset Boulevard and Fountain Avenue, and I stopped at a bar to get a drink. I saw no external signs of what kind of place it was. The interior decoration had a communist theme; there were lots of hammers and sickles in red and gold, but no pictures of political leaders or propaganda posters. The only patrons were men, two aside from me, and they were engrossed in conversation. From the way they interacted, I could tell they were gay. I didn't want to intrude, but their discussion was the only thing happening at the bar, and I tried to eavesdrop. I could make out very little, just a few acronyms of political parties and radical groups. After drinking a ginger ale, I got up to go. I looked for matchbooks with the name and address of the bar on them, but there were none. I wanted some proof that I had found a communist gay bar.

∞

I was happy to have somewhere to stay in Los Angeles, and Moira's parents were perfectly hospitable to me. They lived in a wealthy neighborhood that happened to be on flat land and right in the middle of the city. I had thought that the rich always lived in the hills, at the beach, or in the suburbs, but Hancock Park had been an old-fashioned bastion of power since the time when the most privileged Angelenos fled Westlake (the area around what is now called Macarthur Park) to points west. A generation or two before, they had fled Pershing Square for Westlake. There was so much available space that rich people continued to remove themselves to other parts of town when their surroundings became undesirable to them. Neighborhoods had the potential to change rapidly, upward or downward on the social scale, depending on the economy and the state of race relations in the area.

Moira's father was an attorney with connections in City Hall, and her mother did charity work. Moira neglected to tell me that all four of her sisters would be at home during my stay. In a house full of women who had attended or were attending all-girls' schools, I was a disruptive male presence, and the effect was unnerving. I felt as though I had fallen into a nest of vampires. Each had an agenda: one sister wanted to know how Moira was dressing, and if I thought this was an indication that she had lesbian tendencies; another formed the theory that Moira had developed a taste for Latino men, and this was the true motivation for her political activities; another wanted to know if she was using drugs, and if so, which ones. I couldn't tell what information would be reported back to their parents or shared among the sisters or even told to Moira herself, so I said almost nothing, aside from mentioning her aversion to drugs, a common attitude among leftists. At that time, imprisoning people for their political activities was still widely held to be repugnant to the American legal tradition; consequently, the police generally arrested radicals on drug charges, a practice left over from the hippie era. Leftists abstaining from illegal drugs were much less vulnerable to arrest.

Moira's father, who was rarely home, took me aside one night and asked about her. He was concerned for her safety. Apparently, Moira had not told her parents about her future plans. They pictured their daughter, a tall, pale woman with a shock of platinum hair, as a conspicuous target in the war zones of Central America. I could say little to allay their fears. Her father shook his head. "I hope she's not crazy enough to join a band of guerillas."

I made my best guess: "I think she may be underground, and what she told us is a distraction. A while back, I remember her telling me that 'underground' is not a location, but really describes the management of information. The person going underground cuts off contact with family and friends, and stops all habitual behavior, like visiting favorite places. That way, when law enforcement officers ask questions, everyone tells the truth when they say they know nothing. Moira is probably perfectly safe, hiding in plain sight. She may even be in Los Angeles."

At this, her father looked relieved. "And if she's here, she can always come home if she needs to." He asked, "Do you really think she's in LA?"

"It's certainly possible." I mouthed a comforting platitude because in reality I knew nothing.

∞

Not long after that conversation, I went out to a gay bar. I had heard a name, Roosterfish, and I went to Venice to find the place. I should have known better than to arrive at ten p. m. on a Saturday night. The line to get in stretched around the block. After I parked,

I walked to the end of the line, and I noticed that nearly everyone wore a similar outfit, jeans and a college sweatshirt. There seemed to be three main categories of schools represented: Ivy League, Big Ten, and University of California.

I tried to strike up a conversation with the pair of men in front of me in line, but when I asked them about their uniform—one that I had never seen in a gay bar before—my question was met with a smirk and a laugh. It didn't take me long to figure out the purpose of the uniform on my own. These were all aspiring professional men. They didn't want to waste their time chatting up or fucking or possibly dating someone without a college education. And if it came to finding a boyfriend, a hope that many gay bar patrons nurtured but rarely talked about, it was imperative that this person be of an appropriate, i. e., similar, social status. I felt as though I was seeing a new breed of clones at its point of origin in a small West Coast enclave. I was curious to see if this kind of uniform signaling social distinctions would become a broad trend.

The men in front of me wore sweatshirts from Cornell and UCSD, which is to say they were at the top of the middle of the Roosterfish's pecking order. Perhaps they set their sights on the bespectacled fellow I spotted in line wearing a Harvard Law School sweatshirt. I wondered if it had occurred to them that there was a flaw in the strategy of the gay bar credentialists: anyone with a bit of cash could buy a Harvard sweatshirt, and liars were far from uncommon in the gay scene. I didn't bother myself with such reflections for long. I grew tired of waiting in line and went home. I knew I wouldn't have much luck at this bar anyway. I wasn't wearing a college sweatshirt; in fact, I'd never even owned one.

∞

A week later, I found my first Los Angeles apartment. It was a basement unit, almost a cave, in a bungalow court on a hillside in Los Feliz. The apartment seemed like an afterthought, and possibly wasn't legal, but the rent was very cheap for such a convenient neighborhood. When my upstairs neighbor wasn't getting laid—she played sentimental music at a considerable volume as prelude and accompaniment to her amorous activities—it was a quiet place. Few of my neighbors knew I existed. When I met them by chance, they treated me like the neighborhood troglodyte. Occasionally, someone would say, "I didn't know a person lived down there," but mostly people would keep their remarks to themselves and leave me in peace, and I liked it that way.

The first place in the neighborhood I visited was the communist gay bar, only about a mile away from my new apartment. I arrived at the corner of Sunset and Fountain a little after nine p. m. I hoped to see more than a crowd of three in the bar. When I reached the place, I saw an official notice pasted onto a padlocked door. It had closed shortly after my first and only time there. If I hadn't seen it with my own eyes, I would have dismissed the bar as a fantasy. I never did find out its name.

∞

While I was still staying in Hancock Park, I started going to the New Beverly Cinema, a revival house nearby. Moira had mentioned it when we were at school together, and while their programming was not always to my taste, I enjoyed seeing old movies projected on screen.

On a slow night, I told the beautiful ticket taker that she looked like Anna May Wong in *Shanghai Express*. She smiled and motioned for me to enter the theater. After that, she always let me in to see movies free of charge, and little by little I got to know her. She told me her name was Anne. Her ethnicity was ambiguous, and her style looked like a cross between traditional Chinese concubine and dominatrix. She seemed to hate attention from men, yet she had cultivated a look that was hard to ignore. Anne often carried a copy of *Psychopathia Sexualis* by Richard von Krafft-Ebing with her and could cite case histories the way fanatical Christians cite chapter and verse of the Bible. She was a complicated woman.

Anne told me stories about the New Beverly's patrons, who were often a spectacle in themselves. One of the regulars was Lawrence Tierney, who had played a handsome and terrifying lout in *Dillinger* and *The Devil Thumbs a Ride*. He always came to the theater when one of his films was playing, and the management let him hold court and sign autographs. He brought headshots that were over forty years old and bore almost no resemblance to the person he had become after decades of hard living. He didn't seem to mind. "I look like a fag in those pictures," he told Anne, "too pretty." Sometimes Tierney showed up drunk and belligerent at random screenings. Since he was a big man, no one on the theater staff was strong enough to evict him physically. People had to put up with his heckling until he passed out.

On one of those horrible nights, Tierney came to a screening of *L'Atalante* by Jean Vigo. I was there because Anne had called me to say its audience included some of the best looking men she had ever seen, and I had to check them out for myself. Why Tierney came was anyone's guess, and as soon as he realized that the program was a French film from 1934, he started bellowing. A man who thought he was helping asked if he could call a cab, and Tierney tore into him. "What are you, some kind of cocksucker trying to get in my pants?" The man slunk away.

Tierney was so put out that he didn't take a seat but stayed in the lobby. I was happy not to hear his comments shouted at the screen. After I watched about a half hour of the film, I left to go to the toilet. At the doorway, I saw Anne struggling with Tierney, trying to scratch his face. He was throwing his weigh against her, pinning her to the wall. He said to her, "I bet you want to get raped in the men's room. Come on, let's go fuck in a stall." Anne screamed.

I yelled in my toughest tone of voice, "I'm calling the cops now!" I went to a pay phone and pressed zero.

Tierney looked back and saw I wasn't kidding. He decided to make a run for it, and left as quickly as he could get his lumbering girth through the door.

Anne collected herself and smoothed her hair in the men's room mirror. "Thanks," she said.

From that night on, Tierney was banned from the New Beverly, until he wasn't anymore. When he returned, he made sure he hung around only on nights when Anne wasn't working.

I continued to go to the New Beverly long after I moved to Los Feliz, even though it wasn't very convenient for me. When I was completely broke, Anne would give me food. I ate popcorn and hot dogs from the concession stand for dinner, then she would steal candy bars for me to eat for breakfast the next day. The only meal I would have to worry about was lunch. Sometimes I came to the theater for food and wouldn't watch the movies. This annoyed Anne, but she fed me anyway.

∞

At that time, I held Rainer Werner Fassbinder in the highest esteem among directors. I was lucky to have seen many of his films in college. The situation for seeing his work in Los Angeles during the years following his death was not very good. The many films Fassbinder made for German television were almost completely inaccessible then, but at UCLA I managed to see one of the best, *I Only Want You to Love Me*.

In the film, a young man named Peter works like a maniac to build a house for his ingrate parents. Nothing pleases them, and he goes deeply into debt to achieve some status in their eyes. He moves to Munich (the most expensive city in Europe in the mid-1970s) and works in construction for a cheapskate boss who refuses to give him a raise, despite repeated requests made on his behalf by the foreman. Peter puts in many hours of overtime so he can afford to bring his girlfriend to the city and furnish a nice apartment. He lives beyond his means, always buying expensive objects to gain approval and love. Peter finally cracks up and kills a man, not his father, who probably deserves it, but a local café owner who resembles his father. The film is based upon the true story of some poor soul sentenced to life in prison for murder.

I drew two insights from this film: first, wage labor is a scam, and the irrational spending encouraged by consumer society only serves to imprison working people in debt; second, Fassbinder had great taste in men. The man playing Peter (Vitus Zeplichal) is young and fresh and beautiful when he shows himself naked in a sex scene with his girlfriend. But it is Armin Meier, playing the foreman on the construction site, sporting a perpetual three-day beard and looking a bit like a refugee from the Balkans, who almost steals the film. A former butcher from Lower Bavaria, Meier was one of Fassbinder's lovers who also appeared in his movies. Another was El Hedi ben Salem, who played a Moroccan guest worker in *Ali: Fear Eats the Soul*. Both he and Armin Meier committed suicide before Fassbinder's own death in 1982. The man must have been a monster.

I read as much about Rainer Werner Fassbinder as I could lay my hands on, preferring factual, biographical accounts, even gossip, over academic writing. As an undergraduate, I had been taught that biography was irrelevant to literary interpretation. It was all about "the text"; consequently, when left to my own devices, my appetite for forbidden material was insatiable. I wanted to solve the mystery of Fassbinder, which as I saw it, came in two parts: what was his psychology, and how had he achieved his meteoric success? I soon learned that the two questions were closely intertwined.

Born a month after Germany's unconditional surrender, Fassbinder grew up neglected by parents who had bourgeois advantages but who didn't know how to live. His father, a doctor, treated the prostitutes of Munich's red light district until he lost his medical license due to alcoholism. Then he became a slumlord, renting substandard housing to foreign guest workers from Mediterranean countries. Both foreigners from the south and prostitutes would feature prominently in his son's subsequent work. As a teenager, Fassbinder and a friend briefly became prostitutes, and he familiarized himself with the sex act as power relation and financial transaction, also crucially important to his films.

From adolescence, Fassbinder wanted to become a director, and in the face of rejections from film school, he decided to learn by doing. He took over a theater group and started making films using this troupe of actors as his stars. His immense energy and drive, as well as his infantile stunts to get attention, held everyone in awe. They were weak, and he was strong.

During this early period, Fassbinder directed as many as seven features a year, and once his reputation for finishing provocative films on small budgets had been established, he experienced little trouble finding backing for more. He worked feverishly—a friend said that Fassbinder wrote the entire script of *The Bitter Tears of Petra von Kant* on a flight from Frankfurt to Los Angeles—and all aspects of his personal and professional life tended towards chaos.

The mass media imposed its normative standards by focusing on Fassbinder's leading ladies, particularly Hanna Schygulla, who was a star from the beginning and always maintained a professional relationship with the director. I was more interested in the unofficial story, Fassbinder's messy relationships with men, especially Armin Meier. Fassbinder, who never spent a single day on a regular job, had a passion for working class men, with consequences that were ravishing in his films and disastrous in his personal life.

Armin Meier was the product of the Nazi *lebensborn* program, an attempt to breed racially pure Aryan children and indoctrinate them from birth into National Socialist ideology. After the war, these children, when their origins were revealed, became social outcasts, and many, like Meier, ended up in orphanages. Meier was illiterate, and he was not taught to read even after being adopted as a teenager by a Bavarian doctor who used young Armin as a personal servant and sexual plaything.

In 1974, Fassbinder extricated himself clumsily from a relationship with El Hedi ben Salem (who was married to a woman and had children), and soon afterwards met Meier and immediately fell in love with him. At first, Meier assumed the role of servant, but Fassbinder had other designs: believing he had met his Marlene Dietrich, he cast Meier in a number of films. This project was doomed to failure, due not only to Fassbinder's extreme and histrionic way of dealing with those close to him, but also to Meier's inadequacies. This child of the master race couldn't act. He had a handsome face, a resonant voice, a bulging crotch, and a shapely ass, but he couldn't read a script. He would have been more at home in pornography, exploited along with other humans who were at once genetically superior and, in the eyes of respectable society, absolutely disposable. When breaking up with Meier, Fassbinder made one last sadistic gesture: he sent a letter written in a complex, elevated style, a message the recipient couldn't understand. While Fassbinder was in New York, finding a new lover and preparing to celebrate his thirty-third birthday, Meier stayed at home and took the break up letter to mutual friends to ask them what it meant. That weekend, he committed suicide.

My other great love in cinema, gay pornography, was much more available to me than Fassbinder films during my first years in Los Angeles. Several video stores in my neighborhood carried large selections, and as soon as I had settled into my new apartment, I bought myself a used VCR and began watching what had been so inaccessible to me during the preceding years.

I felt a sense of mourning while watching this material, not only in the obvious way—many porn performers had died or would soon die of AIDS—but in another way as well: the porn industry itself was dying. My regular consumption of porn videos began during the absolute nadir of their production. There is not a single video from the latter half of the 1980s I would recommend on its aesthetic merits, and I'm not aroused by any of them, either. For me, everything started going to hell when porn was no longer produced on film.

Beginning in the late-1960s, gay pornos were generally shot on 16 millimeter film. The expense of film stock forced directors to consider the staging of dramatic action, camera placement, and lighting. After the transition to video occurred in gay porn, very few directors put any energy into making interesting films. They could be careless because there were always plenty of inexpensive tapes to burn. Every director in the industry worked in smeary, low-resolution NTSC video, which is terrible at capturing flesh tones. No one in the United States shot commercial gay porn on film after 1985.

1985 was also the year that gay porn actors began shaving their bodies. Formerly, men in gay porn had natural body hair. They looked mature and masculine. Many groomed themselves as clones. With short hair and prominent moustaches or closely trimmed beards, the clones' uniform appearance gave them the look of interchangeable parts in a giant human machine devoted to getting as much sex as efficiently as possible. The AIDS epidemic in America struck the gay clones early and virtually eradicated their numbers. By the mid-1980s, to adopt the appearance of a clone was to claim membership in a group associated with sickness and death. Many gay men at that time, particularly those in the porn industry, wished to emphasize youthfulness and health. All that body hair seemed dirty and unhealthy, a reminder of the risks they took with their bodies.

The risks were very real, if still rather poorly understood. In those days, AIDS treatments were often as fatal as the illness itself. An effective HIV test was not developed until 1986, five years after AIDS was first described in the medical literature. Although safer sex guidelines had been devised and were widely publicized, gay men did not always follow them. As the 1980s wore on, hardly any urban gay men in America could plausibly claim ignorance of AIDS or the importance of their HIV status. And yet the gay porn industry still required its performers to have sex without condoms until the end of the decade. The performers from that period tended to be older men, survivors from another era, some of whom could be seen getting progressively more ill with every video, and younger men too desperate, careless, or self destructive to find work elsewhere.

I hated seeing these things as they were unfolding, and I certainly didn't find them sexually exciting, yet they were painfully apparent in the porn that was produced during my young adulthood. Consequently, I always associated images of sex with a backward glance. Practically from the moment I first saw sexually explicit films, my viewing habits were an exercise in nostalgia.

FIVE

Frustrated that my only experiences with naked men in Los Angeles had so far been through watching videos, I resolved to make another foray into a gay bar, this time in West Hollywood. I took a chance on Wednesday night, when there would be fewer tourists around, and I chose Rage on Santa Monica Boulevard. A completely conventional gay bar of the time, with house music and occasional wet underwear contests, Rage didn't live up to its "edgy" name at all.

I made a few attempts to converse with my fellow patrons, but most of these went nowhere. I overheard references to a "De Grassi High," and I thought it odd that so many people in a big city happened to have attended the same high school. Later that night I was informed curtly that people were talking about a television show. I never felt tempted to dance, because I didn't recognize any of the songs. To me they were all indistinguishable. When an especially annoying song played, I said something disparaging about it to my neighbor at the bar. He turned to me and said, "Don't be such a bitter Betty. Why don't you go hang out at Club Fuck?"

I responded, "I'd love to. Where is it?"

He said, "Somewhere in Silverlake," and shot me a look of contempt before turning his back on me.

∞

Club Fuck, as it turned out, was not far away from where I lived, and took place regularly at Basgo's Disco in Sunset Junction, the area where Santa Monica and Sunset Boulevards merge. It was something new: a club mainly for the people some called modern primitives, who had become more numerous in the preceding years. During the late-1980s, it was possible to claim a degree of specialness for oneself with body modifications and tattoos; the world had not yet seen many generations covered in piercings and ink. Outsiders to the scene assumed that the modern primitives were changing their appearance drastically to rebel against their parents, but I noticed more serious intentions. Anyone with ambitions beyond being seen and getting laid invariably set about looking for historical antecedents and cross-cultural parallels.

The men of Club Fuck were stunningly beautiful, and I felt abashed in their presence. The most beguiling of them accentuated their resemblance to figures of the Maya nobility as seen in Pre-Columbian artworks, with remarkable profiles, large plugs in their earlobes, and hair done up in topknots. It was a look I recognized from an archaeology class I took in college, but for these men, the connection was much more direct. I doubt anyone resorted to binding their foreheads, as their ancestors had done, but some of the things I saw at Club Fuck reminded me of the penis perforations and hallucinogenic enemas the Maya used to induce visionary trances. Around midnight, someone would perform an ecstatic ritual or extreme action involving the body. I saw more than one spectator become overwhelmed and pass out at the spectacle.

I had enough in common with the people in the scene to enjoy my time visiting, but ultimately, I was only a tourist, if a sympathetic one. I was certainly a pervert, but I wasn't comfortable announcing it to everyone who saw me. I suppose my unwillingness to undergo painful bodily transformations to fit into this milieu could be understood as being "in the closet." If so, I plead guilty. I had a recurring nightmare in which I covered myself with the tribal tattoos fashionable at the time, then woke up twenty years later to discover that I looked perfectly ludicrous.

∞

I learned that two sex clubs were also fairly close to my apartment: Basic Plumbing and Exxile. The former, though it had an intriguing name, didn't interest me. Most of its patrons came from Cuffs, the darkest gay bar in town, the bar of last resort. If a guy couldn't find sex there, he could cross the street (and risk a jaywalking ticket, or worse, being hit by a speeding car) to go to Basic Plumbing. Just a few doors down was Exxile, an innocuous looking pink stucco building; inside was a scene that I preferred. On weekend nights, after a drink at Cuffs, I would sometimes walk down the block and cross the street at the traffic light where Fountain turns into Hyperion.

Exxile was an ideal place to find sex, but what went on there was usually not for me. I figured that most men turned off part of their brains to enjoy anonymous sex completely; I was never able to do that. I liked having a story, a voice, or at the very least a name to connect with a man. I would have avoided sex clubs entirely if it weren't that Exxile, of all the gay places in town, played the music I liked best. I knew Adam the DJ, and I would sometimes be bold enough to make requests. His playlist was extremely eclectic. He realized that no one came to Exxile to dance, so he could get away with playing almost anything. I once heard the tail end of a rare La Monte Young recording as I was arriving. (That would have been appropriate, since Young had graduated from John Marshall High School, just over the hill from Exxile.) I also heard Nirvana's debut album *Bleach* for the first time there. I preferred rock'n'roll to the wailing divas heard at most gay bars, and so did Adam, though he did have a weakness for Yma Sumac. I never tried to initiate anything with him. He might have been open to a little play, as long as it didn't last longer than the side of a record. He was, after all, working at a sex club.

∞

At home one night I heard a very loud metallic sound, not exactly a crash, but more of a scrape, without the screech of tires. I went outside to see that my car had been destroyed while it was parked on the street. I found out the next day that the vehicle was a total loss. At first I couldn't imagine living without a car, but when I got a check from the insurance company, I never managed to use it for its intended purpose. I was too strapped for cash and too lazy to purchase, register, and insure a car in California. The car I lost was ill-suited to the demands of Los Angeles roads anyway, and I couldn't afford the sort of air conditioned sensory deprivation chamber that made commutes of several hours pleasant for suburbanites.

I decided, though I didn't recognize it as a decision at the time, that I would see what my life in Los Angeles would be like without driving. I remembered a bit of dialogue from *Repo Man*: "I do my best thinking on the bus. That's how come I don't drive, see? I don't want to know how. The more you drive, the less intelligent you are." A madman says these lines next to a burning trash can in the film. He is one of the untouchables of Los Angeles, a non-driver, and possibly homeless, too.

Leaving the ranks of drivers went against the grain of my upbringing. Some of the factories in my hometown did subcontracting work for the auto industry. Buying American cars as often as possible was considered something like a duty, and a necessity as well, because every car exposed to the elements (and the salt used to melt ice on the roads) rusted out eventually. I was convinced that privately owned transportation was a scam. I sometimes pictured a giant octopus stretching across the Midwest, its head in Detroit, and its tentacles at their furthest reach strangling the people of my hometown, including my father. The people I had grown up with talked about cars constantly, comparing notes on various makes and models the way they argued about sports teams. I wanted nothing to do with all that.

Being a pedestrian forced me to learn my adopted city's geography by traversing it slowly. This had the added advantage of exempting me from any event I felt like skipping, and my new social status (or lack thereof) selected my circle of friends. When I told new acquaintances that I didn't own a car, some would look at me as though I had just announced that I needed to make a long distance call to Jupiter. These people did not become my friends.

I thrived without a car. I didn't become a screaming fiend behind the wheel, and I got a little exercise. My day-to-day reality was simplicity itself: if I wanted to go anywhere, I had to do some walking. The weather was so beautiful that a walk to any destination, usually a bus stop, was relatively pleasant.

I preferred the rainy winter days, when no pedestrian in his right mind would leave home unless absolutely compelled to do so. My first winter in Los Angeles, the rain poured down for a week at a time, sometimes carrying soil from the hills with it. The streets running south from Griffith Park became rivers. On sunny days, I might think it more appropriate to go outside and make something of my life. On rainy days, I felt no guilt about staying in bed reading. I would finish a book, usually a modern novel, in a single day. Nonfiction took longer; *The Decline and Fall of the Roman Empire* lasted an entire month.

Books were not easy to come by then, because Los Angeles didn't have a decent public library. It wasn't the city's fault; one fine day in 1986, an arsonist started a fire in the stacks of the main library downtown, and hours passed before it was completely extinguished. In the end, the books that weren't burned had been too water damaged to use. When I arrived in Southern California, the region's largest library had already been closed for some time and there was no indication of when it would reopen.

In isolation I developed my own social theories, which I later had occasion to recant, but which I believed at the time. I conceived the idea that people who didn't read simply didn't exist as humans. What they were exactly, I wasn't sure. After further interaction with the world outside my door, I admitted that my position was a bit extreme. I became familiar with three categories of non-readers who were clearly human: the illiterate, a very large group, including many who had passed through California's public schools; the proletarians, whose work and family lives took such a great toll on them that they didn't have a single spare moment to themselves to read and think; and finally, those who enjoyed the privilege of literacy, enough spare time to read, and adequate resources to buy books, but who chose to exist in an ambulatory yet mentally vegetative state. I held this last group in a contempt that I didn't bother to hide. Whenever I entered the house of an acquaintance, I would gravitate to the bookshelves. If I found that this person had no books, I would turn around and leave without a word, taking the next bus back home. After this happened on multiple occasions, I softened my position towards the willfully non-literate: such people actually existed, but they had no inner lives.

I came to these thoughts while patronizing the gay bars of Los Angeles. Without a car, I had no desire to go all the way to West Hollywood for a drink, even if there were a congenial bar there. I stayed in Silverlake and Hollywood, where the bars were rougher than the ones further west. Still, aside from Basgo's on a Club Fuck night, these "alternative" bars were usually pretty awful. If the incessant thumping of the music didn't repel me, then the attitudes of the patrons did. Many of these men would have felt at home among the National Socialists, exercising constantly, seeking to eradicate weakness in themselves and deviance in others, worshiping remote authority figures who rarely, if ever, acknowledged their existence, striving for status and acclaim in a world that regularly expressed its hatred for them. They didn't read anything of consequence, and furthermore, they judged harshly anyone who did. Those who refused to conform to a lifestyle with all the depth and commitment of a television commercial were shunned as "no fun." In retrospect, I can hardly blame these men, whose working lives were undoubtedly hell, and who sought a much needed good time, which often involved losing themselves in a haze of drugs.

∞

My neighborhood had two main bookstores, Chatterton's and Bolzano's. Shoplifters would steal books at the former and then sell them to the latter, which in turn sold them to people like me at a discount.

Bolzano's was a great firetrap of a used bookstore. Shelves stretched way above customers' heads and were separated by very narrow passages. Claustrophobia and aversion to dust prevented me from exploring the further reaches of the store, which were almost entirely in shadow. The most valuable books were kept close to the front, within view of the proprietor, a big bear of a man named Eugene. He wore thick glasses and had a bald spot on the top of his head with a long fringe of hair around it. He had grown a large frizzy beard, more from neglect than intention. On the rare occasions when he left his perch, a high stool with a padded seat, he walked with a limp. Whenever he passed by, I noticed a distinct odor, sweat mixed with something else I couldn't quite place, which indicated to me that he didn't bathe very frequently, perhaps because he was living at the back of his store. I had no clue as to his age. He could have been anywhere from a decrepit thirty to a well-preserved sixty.

Whenever I was in Bolzano's, I would notice Eugene watching me. I thought he suspected me of shoplifting. I bought things infrequently, because even used books were a strain on my budget, and the cheapest fiction titles languishing in the gloom at the back were in rather poor condition. Every so often I would see someone talking to Eugene. I couldn't tell whether he—it was always a man— had come in from the street by chance or was homeless and asking for temporary shelter in the store. With one of these men, the conversation was more personal than usual. I was several shelves away, insulated by hundreds of books, yet I got the feeling that they were talking about me. I returned to the front, and the two of them looked embarrassed and a little pleased with themselves. At that time, I was only dimly aware of my sexual attractiveness, such as it was, but I have since learned that a young white man who is tall, pale, and skinny is exactly what some men want.

One evening near closing time I caught Eugene licking his lips at the sight of me. I found a couple of $2.00 books that didn't look too damaged (Thomas Bernhard and Joe Brainard) and brought them to the front. I wanted to see what Eugene would do. He looked around to check for anyone else in the store, wiped his brow, and said, "If you let me blow you, you can have 'em for free."

The thought of a guy most people would find repellant sucking my cock gave me an instant erection, and Eugene noticed it. He hobbled over to the entrance, turned the sign around to "closed," and locked door. He motioned for me to sit on his stool. I unbuttoned my jeans. I wasn't wearing any underwear. Eugene knelt down and started to nibble at my crotch. His beard tickled my inner thighs. He began to suck my cock, and I discovered he was very good at it, using his hands to jerk me off and caress my balls, and not scraping my cock at all with his teeth. The sight of his bald head bobbing up and down excited me. There was a border of hair sticking up from the neckline of his t-shirt, and for some reason, at the moment I saw it, I came. He swallowed the load of cum as best he could, but a bit spilled onto his face. I didn't tell him about it. The thought of him walking around the neighborhood with my cum in his beard pleased me. He interrupted my reveries when he looked up and said, "Don't forget your books," which was my cue to go.

I said, "Thank you," as he let me out of the store. I walked back home, and the first thing I did when I got there was to throw myself on the bed and masturbate. The moment after I ejaculated, I fell asleep. When I woke up it was the middle of the night. I turned over, switched on the light, and read *Wittgenstein's Nephew*, finishing it at dawn.

After that day, I would return to Bolzano's every week for more books and sex. I became accustomed to Eugene's distinctive smell and began to associate it with pleasure. I started to get curious about the back room, and one day, after an especially good afternoon blowjob, I asked Eugene, "Do you ever get fucked?"

"Hell yeah, but it's been a while…" He looked at his watch, and after a pause, he said, "Come back in an hour and you'll see."

I went around the corner to Chatterton's to kill time. Even though it was the better bookstore in the neighborhood, fancier than Bolzano's at least, it was a wreck. The owner was dying a lingering death, and he let the place deteriorate. It had been over a year since he had ordered new stock, because distributors had cut off his credit. The old stock began to disappear as thieves realized that decent books with resale value were more or less available for the taking. I never availed myself of this opportunity, except indirectly by patronizing Bolzano's.

Finding nothing much of interest at Chatterton's, I walked down Vermont Avenue to Amok Books. I rarely visited since they moved from their Silverlake location, where I had seen an art exhibition by the prolific mass murderer John Wayne Gacy. This show of cartoonish clown paintings had been an early manifestation of the subcultural fascination with serial killers, not as the monsters they appeared to be in the media, but as heroes after a fashion. Their status was obvious to anyone paying attention in Los Angeles, but at the same time, all but impossible to explain to the uninitiated.

The most important precursor of this tendency was the cult film *The Honeymoon Killers*, based on a true story and released in 1970. The producer and director (a gay couple who never made another movie) had intended *The Honeymoon Killers* as an art film, but due to its lurid subject matter, they could only secure grindhouse and drive-in distribution in the US. Later, European festivals honored it, and François Truffaut called it the greatest American film of the era. These distinctions eventually led to its acceptance as a classic.

The killers of the film's title, Martha Beck and Raymond Fernandez, ran a scam defrauding unmarried women they contacted through personal ads. Raymond would marry these women and relieve them of their savings; his lover (and erstwhile victim) Martha posed as his overprotective sister. When one mark became suspicious and threatened to cause trouble, the couple bludgeoned and strangled her. This initiated a killing spree, fueled by Martha's obsessive jealousy of Raymond's fiancées, some of whom he took to bed. In the film, these unfortunate women come across as patriotic ghouls. One of them sings "Battle Hymn of the Republic" in her bath as a prelude to her wedding night; another throws a birthday party for Abraham Lincoln.

On the initial release of *The Honeymoon Killers* during the late stages of the Vietnam War, the film's audience sided with Raymond and Martha, cynical yet passionate grifters who had no tolerance for pious and irritating behavior. To many spectators, the victims were really to blame, as the killers lashed out not at vulnerable American innocents, but at America's false values. This political dimension— publicly denied by the makers of *The Honeymoon Killers*—almost never expressed itself in the acts of real murderers, but for a whole generation of hipster ironists, it served as a comforting myth. I felt a twinge of distaste for these film fans who had never had the slightest contact with actual killers, but at the same time, I felt outright disgust for the moralists who pointed out this contradiction. I came to believe that the debate around these issues ultimately boiled down to aesthetics. As the honeymoon killers throw an assortment of kitsch religious icons into the grave of their first victim, Martha mocks her favorite expression, "Isn't that cute?" It's an example of camp as a way of converting the serious into the frivolous, and seeing everything through the lens of taste.

I had almost memorized Amok's stock: books not only on serial killers but also on UFOs, conspiracy theories, and anarchist politics; a few records by Martin Denny or whatever noise group was currently fashionable—no popular music for them, only easy listening or ear torture—and a few random 8-track tapes; wretched bootleg videos of Andy Warhol films; a bit of collector's kitsch, like shrunken heads, tiki mugs, and school lunch boxes from the 1970s. I occasionally found something to buy there. This time it was a beautiful little book, the Hanuman edition of Jean Genet's *What Remains of a Rembrandt Torn into Four Equal Pieces and Flushed Down the Toilet*. The last word of the title is more polite in English than in French (*chiottes* or shitters), and appropriate in light of Genet's appreciation for the visceral qualities of painting. His highest tribute was declaring that the bodies of Rembrandt's subjects looked as though they were warm and smelled, they digested and shit.

I walked back to Bolzano's. I found the door locked well before closing time. I knocked, and someone I recognized as a friend of Eugene's opened the door. He was called Bigotes because he had the bushy black mustache of a Mexican *macho*. He wore the uniform of the urban *ranchero* of that time: a very fine cowboy hat, a knockoff Versace shirt in a loud shiny print, blue jeans, a handmade belt with the head of a steer on the buckle, and a pair of well-worn and beautifully made boots. He had dark brown skin and a lot of chest hair spilling out of his shirt, which was unbuttoned practically to his navel. Bigotes led me back to the office at the end of a dark and narrow corridor lined with books.

In the office I saw Eugene sprawled naked on a dirty mattress with no cover. Eugene had a fat, pale body, almost like a lump of lard, a very hairy back, and a rather smooth ass. Bigotes helped me off with my clothes and started sucking my cock. It felt so good that I immediately understood why he had grown the mustache. Eugene groaned in a way that said "fuck me," so I pulled my cock out of Bigotes's mouth and knelt down behind Eugene. I slipped my cock inside Eugene's ass. It had already been lubed up. I pumped his ass, which was surprisingly loose. I looked down at my cock going in and out, and I noticed a white foam around his hole. "Sloppy seconds," I thought. Bigotes had fucked him and come in his ass while I was around the corner. I looked over at him, and he gave me a sheepish grin. Bigotes was fully dressed and watched intently as I fucked Eugene. Almost at the point of coming, I pulled my cock out of Eugene's ass and moved up to his head. I grabbed it and made him suck me. He swallowed my cock like a starving man. I looked over and noticed that Bigotes had started jerking off. His jeans were around his ankles. The sight of his big brown uncut cock made me ejaculate immediately. I choked Eugene with a huge load of cum. As he coughed and spat, I saw Bigotes shoot a thick white stream of cum into the air as he stared into my eyes.

∞

The next time I went to Bolzano's, it was Friday and Eugene wasn't there. I had never considered the possibility that he would leave the store except to go wherever he slept (and bathed, I hoped). On the stool at the front was Bigotes, an odd choice for a replacement at the desk. As far as I could tell, he spoke no English. I went to my usual spots in the store looking for nothing in particular. I noticed that Bigotes was staring at me. He had unbuttoned his shirt and was running his fingers through his chest hair. I walked down another aisle. I came back around to the front to find him in a completely different posture: he had taken down his jeans and perched on the stool with his ass in the air. Bigotes was so hairy that even though he was naked from the waist down, he looked as though he was wearing a pair of brown pants. I came up to Bigotes and did the first thing that occurred to me; I licked my finger and put it in his ass. He let out a gasp. I said in my rudimentary Spanish, "Ven conmigo."

Bigotes got down from the stool, zipped up his jeans and flipped the sign so it read "closed." Once outside, he locked the front door, which had been open the whole time we were in the store together. There was no conversation, so the walk to my place seemed to take forever. We finally reached my charmless basement apartment, which was only a little nicer than the back room at Bolzano's. I had barely shut the door and Bigotes was all over me. He was even hungrier than Eugene, and I was pleased to find out that he smelled better. He dropped his clothes, belt, and boots next to my front door, and for the next forty-eight hours or so, he remained naked. We spent a whole weekend fucking. I suppose it could have gone on longer, had I not physically thrown him out the door when I had to do an errand on Monday.

Bigotes the *macho* was mostly passive in sex. In his case, passivity entailed rubbing his ass up against me at every opportunity to try to give me an erection. His back was hairless, unlike Eugene's, but one uninterrupted patch of black hair covered his armpits and chest. When he ejaculated, which could happen at the slightest provocation, the sperm sometimes hit his armpit. It once hit the wall.

∞

Over the next few months, I would see Bigotes periodically but without warning. He had no phone, and neither of us drove. Every so often he would just show up at my place ready to get fucked. At some point, he stopped coming. I figured he had moved to another city or gone back to Mexico, because I didn't see him again, not even out of the corner of my eye.

After I fucked Eugene in the back room, he rarely acknowledged me when we saw each other in the store. I managed to have one conversation with him. I brought up Bigotes, whom I hadn't seen in a while. He told me that Bigotes's real name was José, and he came from the Mexican state of Michoacán. He had been working in restaurants, saving money and sending it back home. He got fucked as much as possible in Los Angeles, because he knew he was expected to marry a woman and wouldn't be able to get very much sex with men in Michoacán. I was sad that he had gone, probably forever. I wished I had been able to communicate my appreciation for his presence in my life, but our interactions were fleeting and unpredictable, and I never had a chance. I took some pleasure in imagining José back in his hometown, living in the house he built with money made in the United States, raising a family with his wife, and fantasizing about cock in his idle moments.

SIX

A free magazine called *Frontiers*, published in West Hollywood and distributed at gay bars and adult bookstores around town, came to my attention soon after I found my apartment. It was famous for its advertisements, the only part of the magazine that anyone read. Escorts, masseurs, models—all of these professionals and more appeared in its back pages. Certain older men, not wanting to deal with the dangers of street trade on Santa Monica Boulevard or the intimidating banquettes and mirrors of a hustler bar like Numbers, made use of these ads. I was fascinated by them.

I recognized many adult video performers in the back pages of *Frontiers*. Only the most famous could support themselves from work in the industry alone; everyone else used their performances as calling cards for hustling. Even minor stars had fans wanting in person one-on-one sessions. The pictures in *Frontiers* ads usually came from the videos in which performers appeared at the height of their attractiveness. As the years passed, the pictures didn't change but the performers did, never for the better.

LA Plays Itself, made in 1972, was one of the first porn films I ever saw, and it remained a favorite of mine. I would even go as far as saying that it had been a factor in my decision to move to Los Angeles. The director and star, Fred Halsted, was still around, as his hustler ad in *Frontiers* attested. It featured a black and white picture of Fred naked and in his prime. The musculature of his upper body was perfect without being fussy, as though his physique had happened naturally. His torso was smooth, with only a faint trail between his belly button and pubic hair. The look in his eyes, a slight squint, made him seem serious, as did his mouth resting in a barely perceptible frown. He looked displeased with being photographed, and he held his hands poised to make a fist at a moment's notice. He projected the image of a perfect thug ready to rough up anyone who crossed him. Fred's name and phone number appeared at the bottom of the ad along with the phrase "out calls only."

One night I screwed up my courage and called the phone number. It was long distance to the 714 area code, so I waited until after eleven p. m. I got the answering machine, which played Fred's voice saying, "If you don't have $200 for an hour of my time, hang up and jack off. Otherwise, leave a message." My mind was racing. I figured I could buy an hour with Fred. Isn't that why I was living in Los Angeles, to have sex with porn stars? Such was my train of thought when Fred picked up the phone. He had been screening his calls.

"Hey, what do you want?" he asked. He sounded like he did in his film, but a bit drunker.

"I want to buy an hour of your time," I answered.

"Ah, okay… Umm, I'm staying with my family right now, so I can't invite you over. I'll come to you."

"No problem."

"And I don't get fucked, ever."

"Hmmmm." I should have anticipated him placing conditions on our interaction, but I hadn't, so I couldn't think of anything to say.

Fred, on the other hand, was ready with his next line: "If you want, I can beat the shit out of you."

I didn't want that, so I had to come up with an alternative plan. I thought it was a bad idea to invite Fred into my apartment, but I still wanted to see him. I asked, "Do you know Silverlake?"

"Are you kidding? I invented Silverlake."

He seemed ready to convince me on this point, but I cut him short. "Let's meet at the Crest."

He snorted, "The Crust? That old greasy spoon is still in business? Yeah, sure."

"Be there tomorrow at eight."

"Sounds good. Bring cash."

"See you then." I hung up the phone and immediately went to the drawer where I kept what remained from my insurance check. I still had a little over $400, enough for rent. I decided to solve the problem of next month's rent when it came due. I went out with a few dollars and walked to the nearest adult bookstore, Circus of Books at Sunset Junction. I rented *LA Plays Itself* to prepare myself for my meeting with the film's director.

I watched the tape until the wee hours. It started with *Sex Garage*, a bisexual film that I found hotter as pornography than *LA Plays Itself*. The sight of a guy fucking his girlfriend then being forced to service some dirty longhaired biker really excited me. I jerked off. I fast forwarded through the first scene of *LA Plays Itself*, two men fucking in nature accompanied by Japanese music. It was the second scene I wanted to see more. Fred Halsted plays an older man who picks up a new arrival in Hollywood, a nervous teenager fresh off the bus from Texas. There are shots of Halsted driving down Sunset and Hollywood Boulevards in his Ford Ranchero, street hustlers working the area around the First Baptist Church of Hollywood, sex shops, and graffiti. There are also scenes of hippies gathering in Griffith Park, not very far from where I lived.

Halsted takes Joey Yale, his young blonde lover, back to a crash pad around the corner from the YMCA, where he tortures Yale and fucks him brutally. The off-screen conversation of an older man and a younger man has an uncanny power. I was transfixed by the interplay between the cool bravado of the seducer and the almost childlike pleading of the seduced. Just as the music began to build to a climax, the film came to an end. I could have sworn that LA *Plays Itself* ended with a fisting scene, the first ever in a theatrical film, but the VHS copy I rented cut abruptly to a commercial for phone sex. I thought I had been ripped off and even considered asking for a refund, but by that time, I was tired and it was too late for me to take another walk to Circus of Books. I decided to ask Fred what happened to the film when I saw him.

∞

When Fred walked up to my booth at the Crest, I barely recognized him. He wore his hair slicked back, to give the impression that he was a tough guy, maybe a drug dealer. His body had become bloated, and his face had been ruined by drinking or psych meds or both. He had a slightly crazy look in his eye. He was a bit shaky, and he left his leather jacket on, as though he needed an extra layer of protection. This mischievous country boy seemed to be at the end of his porn career, if not his life.

Fred called to the waiter across the room and ordered a couple of beers, both for himself. I had a grilled cheese sandwich and iced tea. Fred ate nothing but made sure the beer kept coming.

"So… what do you want to do with your hour, hold hands and listen to music?" Fred asked in the good natured drawl of someone who had been raised in California. It sounded self-confident and unhurried, well mannered almost to the point of being meek, yet aggressive when one read between the lines. Few outsiders understood this aggression right away. They thought yokels from the West Coast just sounded gullible and slightly out of it, but they didn't realize that in the long run, this attitude would wear them down more effectively than belligerence.

I had been staring at Fred, and I snapped out of it to see that he was waiting for me to answer his question. I imagined that he had experienced this a lot when he was younger. Even now, he exuded a powerful attraction. He smelled like a gardener who hadn't taken a shower after work, then rode to Los Angeles on his motorcycle. I said as calmly as I could, "I'm not in the mood to get roughed up. I thought I'd interview you instead."

"200, please." I gave him the money, then excused myself to go to the men's room as he put it away. I placed a microcassette recorder on the table between us. I figured he would understand this as a request to record what he said. When I returned to the booth, I switched it on.

I started, "I saw *LA Plays Itself* last night and really loved it, but I jerked off to *Sex Garage*. Is *LA Plays Itself* even a porn film?"

Fred laughed a bit and rubbed his chin. He thought for a moment then launched into his answer: "I wanted people to see it as a real film, not just as a faggot fuck-suck film. I'm happy you can rent it on video, even though I haven't seen a cent from the company that released it. I was always ashamed to show at gay theatres, because they're toilets and because the audience is only gay. I have ambitions, you know." He seemed to come alive while he was speaking. I could tell that he had dealt with interviewers many times before, but it had been a while since anyone had bothered to talk to him seriously.

I asked a rather aggressive question, an obvious one with the intention of getting Fred to talk at length: "If you're so ambitious, why have you made only porn films?"

"I like to make sex films because it gives me an opportunity to state my views. I don't do it for money. Nobody else makes gay films the way I do. I have certain ideas about sexuality. I don't particularly view sex as fun. I don't fuck to get my rocks off. In the best scenes I've ever had, I haven't come. I'm interested in getting my head off, my emotions off, and if I get my dick off, it really doesn't matter that much to me, that's very down on the scale. I'm interested in emotional and intellectual satisfaction—mine."

I asked another aggressive question, "Don't you care about your partner at all?"

"For me it's important who I'm having sex with and how they act and behave. I like to work on them to make them understand who they are. That's my most pleasurable challenge. I love to strip my partner, to get through all his layers and expose him to all his lust and greed and why he's with me. And they find it enjoyable, too, once they realize that I'm setting them free, once they can be honest and admit that they're with me because they want to suck my dick or whatever else I'm doing with them. When you get a guy to that level, then there's no hypocrisy, no nothing. I'm really very good at this, but it doesn't happen every time.

"When I bring a trick to the house, I tell him that if he ever wants to split, the door is there. I want him to know ahead of time where the exit is, because eighty per cent of the people I try to fuck will leave before we get anywhere. They can't take the way it builds up. I'm extremely demanding, and I don't take any bullshit. I never know what the fuck I'm going to do. I just gauge it by the person, whatever it takes to break through the person's shell. If the person responds and I respond to them, I can really beat the bloody shit out of them and enjoy it completely. I tell them that they're with me because they want to be, because they want this done to them, because they want these things revealed to them."

I asked, "Are they afraid you're going to kill them?"

Fred let out a little chuckle. "You should have been with me last weekend. My last friend was a fundamentalist Christian. As we went through the night, I revealed his Christianity to him. As he was eating the shit out of my asshole, I told him that the words of the Lord are written right there, right in my shit. And I told him, you don't say to me 'yes, sir,' but 'yes, sir Lord.' I put him through a revelation to himself."

I became a little giddy at the thought of making a fundamentalist Christian eat shit. I wished Fred had said these things to me when I was in high school, even if he probably would have been arrested for it. I couldn't determine if he was telling me the truth or trying to wind me up, but I didn't care. I smiled and said, "You must be fun on a date."

Without acknowledging my remark, Fred continued his sermon. "Sex as sex is already old. The particular thing that flows through all my films is the abuse of sex. This is a theme which is very heavy in gay minds. Gay people are into abuse. And these ideas are constantly going through my mind at all levels, religious, psychological, sexual and so on. I think the abuse of sex and masochism are very strong subliminal gay themes. I happen to be sadistic."

"What does sadism mean to you?" I asked.

"By sadism I mean the need to dominate another. I can't get along with anyone sexually who doesn't want to be dominated. I can't have normal type sex. I'm about the only person who makes gay films from a sadist's point of view. Almost all gays are masochists, if not overtly, at least subliminally. I find that most gays, even when they're not into it and say that they abhor it, are still intrigued by it.

"Masochism is both physical pain and psychological humiliation. I'm going to write a book one of these days about the beneficial aspect of masochism, because in homosexuals—at least many I've met—there's such a mind-fuck element that goes into gay sex and gay relationships. The biggest gay porno hits always have S&M themes running through them. Most homosexuals really want to be dominated by another male. That key business or the hanky codes that the leather men use, it's all just playing games. You can take any of them and turn them around. At least I can."

There was a lull. I was in awe. I had a first impression of Fred as a hopeless alcoholic with nothing coherent to say, but he had cast a spell over me. If I had been a rich old trick, I would have offered to invest money so he could make a new film. I wondered how many times he had used a speech like this before. It didn't matter to me; I just wanted to hear more. I decided to draw him out on the subject of the ending of LA *Plays Itself*. I didn't have the heart to tell him it had been cut out of the version available at video stores. He probably knew that already. I said, "Tell me something about fisting."

Fred took a breath. "Fist fucking with a man is unconventional and weird. I consider myself a pervert first and a homosexual second. Sadism is more basic to my personality than homosexuality. I had sex with women before I was homosexual and I was sadistic with women. But I'm not bisexual. Women don't enter my fantasy life. Every once in a while some woman I meet will click with me and we'll go off and fuck. It surprises me when it happens, but it does."

I tried to keep Fred on the topic. "I can understand why a bottom wants a fist in his ass—getting fucked by bigger and bigger cocks, then dildos, then who knows what—but what's in it for you?" I noticed that Fred's hands were big and rough, a peasant's hands. He wasn't looking for amateurs as partners.

He continued, "Your intestines are about twenty feet long. Sometimes your hand can come up almost to the heart and you can feel it beating. It's very exciting to feel a person's bodily process all around your arm. It's as though you can feel their very life. You have a man's life in your hand. The feeling of control is incredible." Fred could tell I wasn't squeamish. He smiled and said, "You know, I thought you were some prissy student or something, but you're kinda okay."

I had been so enthralled by what Fred had to say that I didn't notice the tape running out. We had also gone way over the hour time limit. Fred tried to get up from the booth to go to the men's room, but by that point he was so drunk he could barely walk. I helped him make it across the restaurant. I felt a bit of panic. It was a great conversation, but I had to bring it to an end. I got the sense that letting him stay the night with me would invite drama I didn't need and would probably ruin everything.

I decided to take Fred to a motel a couple of blocks down Sunset from the Crest. At first, he balked at letting me drive his big pickup truck, which was a standard shift, but the moment he got into the passenger seat, he passed out. I checked in at the front desk and paid for a room on the first floor. I had to slap Fred a few times to wake him up, but we finally managed to get inside. He collapsed on the bed and quickly started snoring loudly. I couldn't think of anything else I could do for him in that state. I put his keys on the nightstand and left him there.

It was well past midnight when I walked the mile or so back to my apartment. To keep myself company, I played the recording I had made of Fred. It started with something I never heard Fred say. He must have recorded it while I was in the men's room. It was an introduction of sorts to the whole evening: "I tried to make it with a guy a few months ago. We started out and everything was going fine. Then he said, 'Haven't we met before?' I said no. He said, 'I've seen you somewhere.' I knew what he was leading up to. I said that I used to know the guy in *LA Plays Itself,* but I don't know him anymore. After that, I lost all interest in the guy. The point is, I don't want to do a performance for anyone."

SEVEN

I was broke, and loath as I was to find gainful employment, I had to get hold of money somehow. I had no hope of a serious career; as many of my generation said, the baby boomers got all the good jobs. I wasn't motivated enough to dislodge any of my elders from their positions, and I didn't have the requisite entrepreneurial spirit to go into business for myself. I also happened to arrive in California during the state's first major economic recession since the 1930s.

I decided the most painless path was to become a video store clerk. It would require dealing with the public, a task to which I was temperamentally unsuited, but at least it would provide me with free rentals. During the VHS era, corporate chains dominated the market. At the end of the 1980s, a new Blockbuster Video opened every seventeen hours, a statistic that terrified the proprietors of independent stores. The only way for them to make a profit was to carry titles the chain stores wouldn't; in almost every case, that meant porn. The place where I found a job, Videoactive, relied heavily on this strategy for its economic survival. It had a huge selection of gay porn and not much else. People would walk in asking for recent mainstream releases, and when they found that the store didn't have them, they would quickly go elsewhere. These customers felt more comfortable in another store nearby called Video Journeys, which also carried gay porn but hid it in a closed back room, and was conveniently located next to an overpriced supermarket. Videoactive was located next to a gym known for its steam room and scantily clad patrons.

Videoactive's customers provided the employees with plenty of amusement and irritation. When a membership card was scanned, messages would sometimes appear on the computer, which was positioned on the counter so that only the clerk could see the screen. Most were notices of late fees or expired credit cards. Some were character sketches of the more problematic customers. Examples included "mean bastard"; "drives a Jaguar and tries to avoid paying"; "smells bad—don't get too close"; and the one every employee dreaded most, "returns greasy tapes."

The porn tapes at Videoactive all bore a label that read "$5.00 cleaning fee." When a customer returned a tape covered with lube, the clerk had the unenviable task of informing the customer that he—it was never a she—had to pay an extra $5.00. The men who were embarrassed quietly paid; others were not so cooperative. One especially difficult customer (the "mean bastard") would often return greasy tapes, and argue that it wasn't he but a previous customer who was to blame. From the smirk on his face I could tell that he got a sadistic thrill from forcing a lowly clerk to deal with the residue of his masturbatory rituals. One Tuesday morning I had a heated exchange with the man, and I informed him that what he said was impossible. He was the first person to rent the tape in question; in fact, he had been the first one to rent most of the gay porn videos displayed in the store. Apparently, my comment struck a nerve, because he shut up and never bothered me again.

This customer was humiliated to be reminded that he was also what I called a Monday man. Videoactive made new gay porn tapes available on Monday mornings, and a small group of men came into the store as soon as it opened to check them out. They rented large stacks of videos and returned them early the next morning, then promptly rented the videos that the other Monday men had grabbed before they did. This pattern of rentals and returns continued for a few days, until every Monday man had seen all of the new porn videos. I never saw any of them rent a title that was over a month old. I wasn't brazen enough to ask, but I suspected that this was because the Monday men had already seen every single gay porn tape on the shelves of Videoactive.

These customers constituted a group only to outsiders who noticed the similarity of their behavior. Even though they had a common interest, they never met to talk about what they saw or coordinate their viewing habits to avoid conflicts over new tapes, at least as far as I could tell. Every once in a while a Monday man would ask impatiently who had rented a particular title, but I was not allowed to divulge that information. I thought this person's identity would have been obvious anyway. They were such a small group that I assumed they all knew each other, but actually, these men couldn't bring themselves to acknowledge their fellows. I never overheard discussions of any substance between them. Each was alone in his obsession.

∞

I didn't make fun of the Monday men as some of my coworkers did, because in a way, I was as lonely as they were. I had trouble meeting men with whom I had anything in common, so I gave up on that as a goal for my excursions to gay bars. I began to patronize a place called the Blacklite on Western Avenue near Santa Monica Boulevard. I didn't expect to meet a boyfriend or engage in profound conversation; I went there to have a good time.

The Blacklite accepted everyone regardless of social class or race, and the drinks were cheap. Every day by early afternoon, the career alcoholics would take their places on the stools at the bar. The tables didn't fill up until much later. At night, the Blacklite provided a meeting place for the transvestite hookers who worked in the area and their proletarian clients, mostly Mexican men with wedding rings.

Every so often, Goddess Bunny would show up. She was an underground personality, having appeared in a few independent films, and she was a regular at Club Fuck. I first saw her in a Joel-Peter Witkin photograph. She was banned from sex clubs for being disruptive, and I imagine the more respectable gay bars gave her the bum's rush. At the Blacklite, she was a celebrity.

Goddess Bunny had been confined to a wheelchair since childhood because her emaciated limbs barely functioned. She never explained how she came to look the way she did, but I had heard that Bunny was born with polio, and after unsuccessful treatments by several quack doctors, her mother, a fundamentalist Christian monster who was probably bitter that her religion forbade her from having abortions, gave her child up for adoption. She spent a horrific childhood in various orphanages and foster homes. Goddess Bunny herself volunteered little about her past or her family; no one even knew her real name.

One night I sat at her table while she held court, regaling us with the story of tricking with a local newscaster. As she spoke, a strap of her gold lamé gown fell and showed her bony, concave chest. A fan sitting next to her put the strap back on her shoulder, and in the pause she glanced over at her rival of the evening, Victoria, who was at a neighboring table.

Victoria came from Cuba, and unlike Goddess Bunny, she told anyone who would listen her life story. She had arrived in the US without a cent and had to hustle to make her way in the world. She sent all her spare money home to her family in Havana. They had been led to believe that she was a successful nightclub performer. The reality of her existence was far less glamorous: she was a street prostitute in Hollywood. She described herself with the wonderful Spanish word *sinvergüenza*, meaning "shameless," which she brandished as a badge of honor.

That night, Victoria wore transparent acrylic platform shoes and a white knit mini skirt. She had applied garish orange pancake makeup to her face, and it was starting to run a little. It had obviously been quite a while since she was able to touch up her lipstick. The poor creature did what she could to hide the jagged, masculine features that other hookers cruelly called *cara de culo* (ass face). In defiance of her detractors, and to draw attention away from her face, Victoria showed her shapely behind as often as possible. I regularly saw her wearing a leather miniskirt so short that her cheeks were exposed. This outfit drew unwanted attention from the police, especially when she ventured more than a block or two away from the easternmost part of Santa Monica Boulevard, where the cheapest street hustlers plied their trade.

Goddess Bunny was about to launch into another story when we heard a crash. Victoria broke a beer bottle against a table top and wielded it at her companion. She screamed, "Just because I sell my body doesn't give you the right to touch me any time you want!" She abruptly got up, stormed through the door, and stuck out her thumb to hitchhike down Western Avenue. The man who provoked her wrath tried to sneak out, but as there was only one door to the Blacklite and Victoria was standing directly in front of it, he was hard to miss. She took the opportunity to scream insults at the man. Once she had calmed down a bit, Victoria came back into the bar and gave her best interpretation of wounded pride.

Goddess Bunny, who had no interest in this spectacle, turned to me and said, "I have to crap, and you gotta help me."

"Um… okay," I said, as I looked around, seeing no one else at the table. The others had gone over to Victoria in the aftermath of the fracas. I followed Goddess Bunny as she maneuvered her electric wheelchair to the rest room, a large space that was protected by a locked cage. (I wondered if the bar had been a pawn shop in earlier decades.) I opened the sturdy metal door for her, and once inside, she shimmied out of her lamé dress quickly and skillfully. It was up to me to lift her skinny frame and pull down her panties. I discovered that she had an uncircumcised penis of greater than average size and large pendulous testicles. I placed her on the toilet. In all innocence, I assumed that I was done with the job at that point, so I made my way to the door.

"Wait a minute!" Goddess Bunny shouted. "You have to wipe my ass."

Holding my breath, I took a wad of toilet paper and did as she told me. I then flushed the toilet, helped her get dressed, and placed her back in her wheelchair. She thanked me, and I felt a new respect for this luminary of Los Angeles nightlife, whose simplest bodily functions required the assistance of people she barely knew on a constant basis.

I opened the door and practically ran into Al, who was having an animated conversation in Spanish with Victoria just outside the rest room. I wondered how much of the evening's drama he had seen. Goddess Bunny shouted, "Coming through!" as she drove back to her table.

Al motioned for me to join him in the rest room. I entered behind him and locked the door. I turned around to see Al unbuttoning his jeans and pulling out his penis. He pissed in the sink so that I could get a full view. His penis was spectacular, long and dark brown and uncircumcised. It was also very thick and asymmetrical, almost grotesque in a way I found very exciting. He finished pissing and started to work his foreskin up and down the head of his penis, which started to swell.

Al turned to me and said, "Get on your knees." Without a second thought, I did so, and he approached me with his jeans around his ankles. He took my head in his hands and forced his cock down my throat. I began to gag. He slapped my face and said, "Swallow it." My eyes were watering, and I thought I couldn't take any more. He fucked my face until I began to feel some precum at the back of my throat. Then he slowed down and ejaculated in several spurts. He pulled his cock out of my mouth abruptly, buttoned his fly, and left me on the rest room floor coughing.

It took me a while to collect myself. I felt as though I'd been raped, but at the same time, I thought, "Be careful what you wish for." I stood up to look at myself in the mirror, which had been covered with graffiti and was of little use. Someone knocked loudly on the door and screamed, "If you've got coke in there, I want some." I adjusted my clothes and left the rest room. I nodded to the patron who had been waiting, and he scowled back. Victoria, who was sitting at a table with Al, looked over at me. I got the impression that Al was speaking to her under his breath, but he didn't look in my direction. Victoria stared with her mouth agape.

I went right out the door and caught the bus back home.

∞

The next day I worked a late shift at Videoactive. That night, I saw an obituary for Fred Halsted in a gay magazine I had brought home from work. It said that he had recently killed himself in an apartment building owned by his brother in Orange County. The obituary listed Fred's films and videos, and implied that career disappointment—never being able to equal the success of LA *Plays Itself*—had driven him to suicide. I couldn't say I agreed, but I had only spent one evening with the man.

In a way, Fred's death upset me more than the death of my own father. I was a bit ashamed to admit that to myself. It was a question of expectation: I was unaware that Fred had so little time left to him. If I had known, I would have made more of an effort to see him again. Our interactions haunted me because they were unfinished. My father had spent years obliterating himself, and by the end of his life, the man I once knew had disappeared. He was done, or we were done with each other; at least that's what I told myself. I had experienced myriad disappointments with an addict dad, and I stopped expecting anything from him but an end to the suffering. Perhaps Fred's brother, who had witnessed his decline and was left to clean up the mess after his death, felt more or less the same way about Fred. I thought about the recording I had made of him at dinner and was keenly disappointed that I would never hear his voice in person again. A while later, I was devastated to find out that the brother had thrown away all of Fred's personal effects: films, videos, photo albums, possibly manuscripts and works in progress. This was a fairly typical outcome for the estate of a gay man of that time, especially if he was poor and ill and beyond the pale of polite society.

The events of those days caused me to question what I was doing in Los Angeles. My life had fallen into a pattern of walking to work, dealing with customers and coworkers for eight hours, renting videos, and walking home. I began to wonder how that routine differed from the sort of job I would have had in my hometown. I was experiencing a social life to which I would not have had access there, but I had nothing to show for myself. I decided the best way to get through it—"it" being this life of menial work, lonely evenings, and occasional impersonal sex—was to write. The writing would be more than a diary or letters to friends; it would be something that captured the texture of my time in Los Angeles. I remembered a sentence I'd read in a book by Joe Brainard: "After an unsuccessful night, going around to queer bars, I come home, and say to myself, Art."

∞

I still read on my days off, but my main form of entertainment on work days was watching movies. The proportion of porn videos to non-explicit films I took home was about half and half. As I saw it, the explicit action in videos produced by the porn industry compensated for a lack of same in the product of the film industry. This was first brought to my attention when I saw a double feature of *Alien* and *Aliens* at the New Beverly with my friend Mike, who worked at Amok Books. As we left the theater, he said, "Those films were okay, but they would have been better if there had been close ups of butt fucking in them." It seemed like a throwaway line at the time, but I have since come to consider it a perceptive piece of film criticism. We have all been conditioned to accept a neutered aesthetic in films, suitable to the taste of the aspiring middle class. Queers, race traitors, radicals, atheists—in other words, the most interesting people in society—were excluded from American films when the Production Code was in effect, from 1934 to 1960, and although its proscriptions now sound risible to everyone but members of the Ku Klux Klan, a hangover of this censorship persists to the present day. Even the coarsest American movie exhibits a prissiness with regard to sex. Church ladies in the audience regularly hear the slurping of chest wounds, but almost never have their sensibilities offended by the slurping of a blowjob.

Normally, when people use the word "better" to describe a film, they are referring to production values: the better film is the more expensive one. The logical extension of this position is simply worshiping money. "I can see where the money went," the producer says as a compliment, and an entire team of industry professionals agrees, but there is no obligation for spectators without a financial interest in the film industry to respond this way to its products.

∞

One evening I saw a double bill of free rented tapes from Videoactive: *Latin Cop Sex* and *Suddenly Last Summer*. In the former, a bunch of uniformed men, including one humpy and hirsute man whose English is nonexistent, shed their clothes and suck and fuck for an hour. In the latter, at a place called Cabeza de Lobo, a bunch of kids kill and cannibalize a notorious homo whose face is never seen. He has been paying to suck their cocks all summer; exactly why they would get rid of such a good source of income, no one is sure. None of the characters in the film can talk about these things. They talk around them a bit, and do some strenuous acting, from a script on which screenwriter Gore Vidal labored mightily, trying to bend Tennessee Williams's original one-act play to the dictates of the Production Code, then in its death throes. Katherine Hepburn's character muses about how her unseen, deceased son benefited from "using people as he did," and Elizabeth Taylor's character very nearly says the word "procuress" before her scheduled lobotomy. Hepburn wears a bizarre hat while visiting the mental hospital, and the presence of Mercedes McCambridge lends a peculiar air to some scenes. That's more or less all the film has to offer in the way of thrills.

I couldn't help but think that a little sexual activity might have awakened the characters in this sleepy Mississippi town. (To judge from his short stories, Williams himself would have agreed.) If Montgomery Clift had been allowed to engage on screen in the sort of down and dirty sex he enjoyed while blackout drunk in his personal life, perhaps he never would have become the catatonic wraith who appears in *Suddenly Last Summer*. Playing a psychiatrist, he keeps himself busy in the film by proclaiming his virtue and controlling the libido of Elizabeth Taylor, who nearly bursts out of her clothes.

Though this is a difficult position to defend, I preferred *Latin Cop Sex* over *Suddenly, Last Summer*, chiefly because the former video's star, known only by the name Carlos, resembled Al.

I masturbated to this video thinking of him. I would never even consider paying such a tribute to *Suddenly, Last Summer*.

∞

The mainstream gay porn industry was transformed at the end of the 1980s, but its productions continued to be as pedestrian as ever. This left the market open to small, highly specialized operations catering to very specific sexual tastes with amateur porn and fetish porn. They featured inexperienced performers who usually identified as straight and engaged in sex acts not involving penetration.

Each segment of the porn industry responded to the AIDS crisis in its own way. The big companies eventually "cleaned up" their product by mandating condoms on set, while performers depilated their bodies. Independent producers exploited the appeal of "real men" who couldn't possibly have AIDS, proletarian bruisers with pre-liberation sexual attitudes and foul mouths. The independents' strategy proved to be wildly successful.

My job in a video store had made me think no more highly of work, but encouraged a deep and abiding love of working men, whose images I saw in pornography. I also began to gain an appreciation for videos with aesthetic merits having nothing to do with production values. I saw that just as gay porn had filled certain gaps in mainstream theatrical films, fetish and amateur porn filled the gaps in mainstream gay porn. In preferring adult movies (as the industry called them) shot on film and directed more or less like theatrical features, I risked being just as snobbish as the film reviewers who write rave reviews for "classy" films. These critics consciously or not want everyone to strive for respectability, and in the process, to become pious eunuchs. The major studios of the gay porn industry—bloated, risk-averse, and, in their way, conservative—had a tendency to reproduce similar thoroughly ingrained prejudices.

Small companies governed by eccentric, all-consuming passions served as reminders that many unacknowledged impulses are at play in movies and in the minds of their spectators.

∞

Occasionally, customers at Videoactive would ask me for advice about videos to rent. The questions generally pertained to which tapes contained the specific sex acts they wanted to see. Most gay porn videos clarify this in the title. I especially enjoyed the name of Bob Jones Productions' *Pits, Tits, and Feet*, which would make some of my coworkers cringe whenever I said it.

A number of fetishes or sex acts weren't represented in any video available for rent, due to "community standards" of obscenity. To my knowledge, shit eating scenes were off limits everywhere in the United States, although Christopher Rage produced scat videos and must have sold them by mail order. Some years before, Los Angeles County enacted an ordinance outlawing piss drinking in porn, a rather curious prohibition considering the priority the region's governments placed on water conservation. There was no law against tickling videos, but Videoactive never carried them, because they didn't rent well.

∞

One day a large, attractive Latino man wearing a cowboy hat and shoulder length hair came into the store and went directly to the gay porn. After a few minutes, he showed up at the counter and asked for help. I accompanied him to the corporal punishment section and pointed out which videos contained choking scenes. Then he asked, "Where are the fisting videos?"

"Are you a cop?" I had been advised to take precautions.

He laughed. "No, of course not. Do I look like a cop?"

"No, you look like a *ranchero*, but I have to ask." He smiled. I continued, "We don't have a lot of fisting videos because of potential legal problems. It's a bit of a rip off, really. For instance, Falcon Studios will make two versions of their movies, one with fisting scenes available only by mail order, and another one without them for rental at video stores."

"Damn, that could get expensive." He looked very disappointed.

"But we carry a few videos that happen to have fisting scenes." I showed him *Good Hot Stuff* and *LA Plays Itself*. "I can't guarantee *LA Plays Itself* will include fisting. It should, but the version on the shelf at Circus of Books doesn't. You might be in luck. This looks like an older version of the tape. Maybe the store bought it from the director." I picked up the video and looked at it. "You know, I can't believe I haven't checked that one out myself."

The customer and I walked back to the counter. He wasn't a member yet, so I had to process his application. His name, Raúl Arroyo y Cajahuaringa de Mendoza, was one of the longest I had ever seen. I asked him, "Where are you from?"

"North Hollywood."

I laughed and wrote my phone number on a slip of paper. I passed it to him with his membership card.

E I GHT

The next afternoon, the phone rang and interrupted my reading. It was Raúl. After a preliminary "hello" and "how are you?" he got straight to the point: "You want to fist me, right?"

"Well, yes." I was a little startled.

"I need a day to prepare. Is tomorrow at two okay?"

"Sure. By the way, I've never fisted anyone before," I admitted. He said. "Don't worry, I'll direct you."

I gave him my address, and that was that. Later, I went to Circus of Books and bought some lubricant in powder form, a product originally developed for use by veterinarians. I mixed it with water and put it in the refrigerator. I trimmed and filed my nails. I didn't have rubber sheets, so I gathered as many old towels as I could to cover my bed.

The next day, Raúl arrived later than he promised because he had to borrow his brother's truck, and the traffic from his parents' house to Los Feliz was worse than he expected. His brother knew why Raúl needed the truck, or at least knew that he was going to have sex with a man; he didn't know what kind of sex, though.

Raúl went right to my bed, got undressed, and lay down on all fours. I poured some lube on my hand and started to put my fingers in his ass. It didn't go well. The lube was way too thick. Raúl asked me what proportion of water to powder I had used. I told him and he laughed. I had put about five times too much powder in the mixture. We took a break while I added more water and shook the bottle. Finally I got the lube to the proper consistency, somewhere between saliva and mucous. I had to keep replenishing the supply of lube on my hand, which caused me some concern, but Raúl reassured me that this was normal.

To get my hand inside Raúl's ass, I needed to collapse it a bit, folding my thumb over my palm and bending my fingers slightly to make a shape that looked like a duck's bill. At first the tension in his sphincter muscles was strong, but then it relaxed. He told me not to push too hard as I entered his ass, but to wait for the hole to swallow my hand. I wasn't sure what he meant until it started happening. I applied a gentle pressure, and suddenly my hand was inside his rectum. It felt like a cork popping, but in reverse. Rather than an actual pop, the action made a slurping sound.

After a moment's pause, I started moving my hand around. Raúl's rectum relaxed and I found I had a good bit of room to maneuver. I reached for a way forward with my fingers and discovered it to the left and up from his hole. I encountered what felt like a shelf of muscle that I had to climb and get beyond. Raúl told me to slow down. In a little while, the muscles would relax and I could go further. The less work I did at the beginning, the more comfortable it would be.

During the first session I didn't go much farther than my wrist inside Raúl's ass. He said we should stop and do another session in a couple of days. He gave me a blowjob. He said, "I don't get fucked by cocks. Fisting is the safest sex there is, if it's done well."

"Am I doing it well?"

"You made good progress today."

After taking a shower, Raúl suggested we go out for a late lunch. He hadn't eaten anything that day, and he was famished. We went to a Thai restaurant in East Hollywood, and there we got to know each other a little better.

I asked Raúl about his accent, "Where do you come from? I mean, originally. I know about North Hollywood."

Raúl shrugged and said, "That's a complicated question. I was born in Lima, Peru. Yeah, that's the easiest way to answer that."

"What's the complicated way?"

"From Lima, my family moved to… well, we moved internally for a few years. Then we moved to Central America. Then my family moved to LA and I moved to Washington State. Then I moved to Costa Rica, where I got a degree in sociology, then I moved to California."

I asked, "Were you ever estranged from your family?"

He said, "Not really. At first I was going along with my family, moving around a lot, that's just what I knew. But once I was on my own, I embraced it and kept moving. I went to a seminary in Guatemala, too."

"Does that mean I got a fisting lesson from a priest?" I interrupted. Suddenly I was very curious.

He laughed. "No, I never went all the way. Not with the priesthood, I mean. I did some missionary work in Guatemala, but that quickly turned into community organizing. I didn't have a religious motivation to go to the country. I was never too close to the church. It was there, it was a presence, but it wasn't necessarily something I had to live for every Sunday. Also, I think that the more you become a theologian, the less Christian you are."

"Are you talking about Catholicism?"

"I did that one thing with the Roman Catholic Church, then I worked alongside some evangelical movements, which didn't end well. Then I became involved with the Lutheran Church, which works for me. I've been a little bit all over the place. And my father's a pastor."

"What denomination?"

"Back in Peru, he was with a local denomination. In the United States, he is with the Lutheran Church, but his practice is not particularly Lutheran."

I was perplexed. "I never understood, are you supposed to go shopping for a church and compare the dogmas so you can choose the one that's most appropriate to your beliefs?"

"There are many things I could say to that, but yes. Definitely some people approach it as going church shopping. It's about the feeling and the music. For other people, it's more about 'These are my beliefs. This is where I find myself, theologically. What aligns with this so I don't rock the boat too much?'"

I added, "Some people simply have no choice. They're raised in religion, and they're expected not to question it ever."

Raúl frowned. "People say that when you come from a religious family, like you just fall in line and all do the same thing."

I said, "I expect the opposite, that people from religious families are going to rebel. I was raised without any religion, so for me, this is all quite strange."

Raúl rolled his eyes. "You have no idea."

I told him, "I really understood something when I saw images of Roman Catholic ritual, this incredible luxury that amazes people as a spectacle. Visiting the Vatican, my reaction was, 'These people are the biggest pimps who ever lived!'"

"Oh my God, yes. There's a reason why they wear gilded ponchos. If that isn't a sign of pimp status, I don't know what is."

I said, "I think a certain segment of the population rejects it and thinks it's corrupt, but a lot of people must go right along with it and think this is great."

Raúl shook his head. "I would challenge that. It's just what they know."

I said, "Okay, so the Church's strategy of inspiring awe in the faithful is not very successful?"

"Well, there are things that do it better now. Before, the biggest show you could get every week was going to church. You get the smells, and the shiny things, and you have this religious leader who's sharing a piece of wafer and you think, 'Oh my God, what does this mean?' Getting this shitty piece of wafer, it's so special, I must be lucky."

I smiled and said, "It's not just a piece of wafer. It is literally the body of this naked guy on the cross with a hard on."

"Well, not everybody believes in transubstantiation. For some people it's literally the body, and then for some people, once you swallow it, it becomes the body, and then for some people, it's a symbol. For other people, it's a symbol, but there is a real divine presence, which gets complicated."

I couldn't believe I was discussing theology with a guy I had just fisted. Raúl didn't ask where I learned what I knew about Christianity, so I didn't reveal to him that a lot of my information came from watching Luís Buñuel films. "I'm sure you're aware of this, but when they were debating transubstantiation in the Church, the people who believed that the communion wafer was only bread were called Stercoranists, which translates roughly as 'shit people.' They didn't really exist, but the Church invented them as mythical figures of ridicule. That's what atheists were, too. They didn't really exist at first, but then they became real."

"When we gave them a name," he said.

"Yes, we give them a name, so now they can exist. Like homosexuals, perhaps." Before we embarked on that topic, we ate some of our food, which was starting to get cold.

∞

After a little while, I asked a question I had been thinking about since I met Raúl, "Is there much fisting going on in Latin America?"

"Yes, but it's underground, even more so than here."

"How would you get access to it in Costa Rica, for instance?"

"You have to be extremely blunt and ask, and people will freak out and never talk to you again, or they'll say, 'I don't do it, but I know this guy who does,' or they'll say, 'I'm into it.' You're in a constant process of coming out as a kink person, otherwise you wouldn't be able to do anything."

"I guess that's why you were so blunt with me on the phone. I've never heard anyone say 'you want to fist me' just like that."

Raúl laughed uproariously. "Yeah, I guess that's where I picked up the habit."

"What are the gay bars like in Costa Rica?"

"Very confined, very dark. You go in through a tiny, unmarked door, and you meet your people, and then you go to the back room, where you do your thing. You come out, you have a drink, and you leave, alone or otherwise. Now that I think about it, when I was in Costa Rica, there was a lot of 'gay for pay,' too, which I guess is not uncommon, but there it was a big thing." Raúl looked at his watch and said, "Damn." It was almost dinnertime, and he was expected at home. His brother needed the truck. We paid the check and left right away.

Raúl dropped me off at home and we kissed. I said, "Let's do this again soon."

"Yeah, we should. I'm only here for the summer. In the fall I'm moving to Chicago."

"Why Chicago?" I asked a little incredulously, because the city was inside my imaginary 500-mile circle.

He said, "I'm going to grad school to get a PhD in anthropology."

I felt a little embarrassed when he said this. When I met him, I expected a guy who acted like a cowboy, not an intellectual. I was pleased that I had been wrong to judge by appearances.

∞

The next time I saw Raúl I was better prepared. I mixed the lube properly, and I bought some incontinence pads at the drug store so I wouldn't have to worry about getting a mess on my bed. I hadn't anticipated how much lube I needed to get a fist in an ass; it was a lot.

Raúl told me that the first time I fisted him, I used a technique he hadn't felt before, but since he had been on all fours the whole time during the session, he couldn't say exactly what it was. I had a tendency to turn my hand while penetrating his ass, rather than going straight ahead. I was using the principle of a simple machine, the screw, which turns to penetrate a surface, and is more efficient than a nail going in a straight line and requiring much more force to drive it.

However my technique differed from the usual, it seemed to have been successful. That day I gave Raúl two orgasms. The first time he ejaculated. After that, he needed a rest, and a little while later, he gave me a blowjob. After I came, I asked him if he wanted more, and he said yes. The second time, I went a bit deeper inside his ass. He was more relaxed, and I was able to reach his bladder with my fingers as my knuckles grazed his prostate gland. After I worked his insides that way for a little while, his whole body began to tremble. Afraid that I might be hurting him, I pulled my hand out abruptly, and this caused Raúl to shudder violently and grunt loudly. I remained calm and let him rest. The spasms returned a few moments later, like the aftershocks that follow an earthquake. After the second round of aftershocks, I asked Raúl, "Are you okay?"

"I'm coming," was all he could say. When the most intense waves of sensation had passed, he turned to me and said, "I hate the next man you'll fist."

"Why?" I asked.

"I'm jealous. You're learning very quickly, and by the time you meet that man, you'll be an expert."

"I'm not even sure how I did that."

"Me neither," he said, "but you're good at reading my body's reactions, when to go forward, and when to stop. And when you turn your hand, you drive me crazy."

"I'm here to serve."

"You're not kidding."

∞

After we took a shower, we went to a small neighborhood sushi restaurant. The lunch crowd had cleared out and we had the place to ourselves. I was still curious about Raúl's past, and the conversation practically became an interview, but he didn't seem to mind. I asked, "Did you have anyone you looked up to in your family, like a gay uncle?"

He said, "My godfather, who was also my uncle, was gay. But I don't think I became aware of him as a sexual being until after he passed away. He died of AIDS a few years ago."

"I'm sorry. What was the reaction of your family?" I asked.

"It was very mixed. At first, they wouldn't even talk about it. After he died, people would keep saying that he died of cancer. But my parents, particularly my dad, had been very close to my uncle throughout that whole time. At one point, my mom and I had the conversation, 'This is what's happened to your uncle. This is what it means.'"

"What kind of life did he have?"

"He was an architect. He was also a sculptor. He liked to travel. He took care of his mom, my grandma. He was the single uncle."

"Every family has one." I laughed.

"Or a bunch of them," he said. "My uncle was very gentle. I remember him being very stubborn, too. He was very demanding of himself. That was because my grandfather was an asshole to him growing up, and he imposed these ridiculously high standards on him. I remember my uncle being a very compassionate person. There was this argument about where my grandmother was going to live, with whom, basically. And everyone in the family discounted him because he was single, and he wasn't the kind of person who would take care of anyone. But then the drama got so big that he just stepped in and said, 'You know what? Fuck you all. I'm going to take care of my mom, because you all are more concerned about yourselves.' And he did. I think for the family that was unexpected. Most people characterized him as very selfish, because he liked nice things. And he was an artist."

I said, "If you're an artist, you have to invent an independent life for yourself, and jealous people see this as selfishness."

"Yeah."

I asked, "Did your uncle have a boyfriend?"

"Yes. He would visit, because he was also taking care of his mom. They didn't really share a space as their home, but he was definitely a presence. For me growing up, he was part of the family, just by virtue of him being there all the time. But most of my mom's generation had this argument: Is he family? Is he not family? Why is he here?"

I said, "It's a way of insulting a queer person in a family setting. 'Who are you?' Just asking a question is alienating."

"Yeah."

"The other annoying thing someone can say to two gay people is, 'How did you meet?' If the answer is 'at an orgy,' what do you say?"

He smiled, "As you know, I like being blunt. Just to shock people, I say it explicitly. It's my way of telling them, 'You didn't really want to know this, but now you do. Mind your business.'"

"What was Lima like for your uncle? Was there gay culture?"

He thought for a moment. "My uncle would never take me to a gay bar, because I don't think there was one. Maybe there was such a thing, but in the underground. There were certain queer spaces that my uncle would take me to all the time for lunch and dinner and coffee and ice cream. I felt at home. I understood why later. They were public venues where things happened unspoken, but still happened. People knew that certain cafés were gay gathering spaces."

"It sounds very civilized. Instead of going to a disco where you can't talk to anyone, you're sitting there eating your ice cream, picking up guys."

He said, "My uncle would spend his time off either drawing or reading. He would go into those spaces, meet people, and have conversations about books or buildings somewhere across the ocean, very passionate conversations—that's how I experienced his gay life. And then years later, I came to find out that he was also into another side of the queer community."

"Oh?"

"One day I was talking to my mom, and she says, 'I have a question. It's about your uncle.' I say, 'You knew him better than me, but okay. What can I help you with?' She says, 'It's been years… but your aunt was keeping all of your uncle's stuff, and she was trying to throw some things away. We came across this suitcase with leather jackets and chaps…' And I say, 'Oh, yeah. I know exactly where this is going.' My uncle was definitely into leather, and probably into some exotic sexual practices, too."

I laughed and said, "It runs in the family."

"Right? And then my mom and I had this whole conversation about how my uncle didn't like dance clubs and loud music. I said, 'Well, that doesn't mean he didn't like being sexually adventurous.'"

I asked, "Where would a leather man go to meet other leather men in Lima at that time?"

"I have no idea, but I'm sure, knowing my people like I do, that it was in intellectual circles."

I thought for a moment. "It's funny you mention that because I saw some early issues of *Drummer* magazine recently. The original concept of *Drummer* was that it would be an intellectual magazine and a leather men's magazine, too."

"Oh, wouldn't that be the perfect read?"

"The first editor was a woman in Los Angeles, and she was a friend of Fred Halsted, who made *LA Plays Itself*. She wanted *Drummer* to be a cross between *Evergreen Review* and gay pornography. It's an ideal that's never been achieved. All this was before leather sex got taken over by consumer culture."

"Now it's drag," he snorted.

"Before the leather scene became all about protocol and costume, it was a culture of outlaws. People whose political ideas, sexual practices, and aesthetics were far from the norm had to band together. They were criminals, after all. And it used to be that gay identity was tied to literature. You would live all alone in some godforsaken place, and you would read a book and realize, 'Oh, there's someone else like me.' That hardly happens anymore because people have access to so much media. I also think our society has gotten less verbal. Being the witty queen who could carry on a great conversation used to have a lot of cultural currency, but that's practically forgotten now. Why talk about anything if you can just go do it, buy it, or see full-color pictures of it? I suppose that's progress."

We went back to my place, and I kissed Raúl goodbye, then he drove back to North Hollywood. After he left, I couldn't stop thinking about our conversation. In idealizing a former condition of gay culture, we risked idealizing a condition of oppression. The queers in the ice cream parlors of Lima were very civilized, but they were not safe from arbitrary arrest and imprisonment. Early issues of *Drummer* contained numerous stories of resistance to harassment by the Los Angeles Police Department, which used paramilitary tactics against queers on the slimmest of pretexts.

Over the last few decades, we have exchanged one regime of power—a state apparatus punishing non-conformity—for another regime of power—a liberated consumer culture that does not punish the perverts, but rather, in a multitude of ways, encourages them to conform. Everything has become inverted: in former times, queers engaged in elaborate rituals of conversation in order to have sex with each other; now we engage in elaborate sex rituals so that afterwards, we can have a decent conversation.

NINE

One night I went to the New Beverly to see *Querelle*, based on the novel by Jean Genet. Rainer Werner Fassbinder's most explicitly gay film, it could have been wonderful, but I found it leaden and desperate, an inadequate end to a career that was extreme in many ways. After making over forty features by the age of thirty-seven, Fassbinder probably had no way of surpassing himself, and any last film would have left the audience unsatisfied.

The dialogue of *Querelle* is outrageously stilted, a common problem with Genet adaptations. As an autodidact, Genet wrote in an elevated style that doesn't sound remotely natural, and when translated to film, it becomes even more bizarre. The post-production dubbing necessary for *Querelle*'s international cast—the film was a French-German co-production—only makes matters worse. The man who reads the English language voiceover narration sounds like William Shatner on barbiturates. In one scene, two adults talk about the title character's penis as though it was the first time they ever saw one.

Perhaps Jean Genet's novel is unfilmable; the only great film he was involved with was the one he directed himself, *Un chant d'amour*, a work he later disavowed. The fault may lie with the cinematic medium itself, invented to entertain the proletariat, but acquiring middle class pretentions early in its history, during times of economic crisis when poor people could not afford even a nickel. Jean Genet was born very poor, and remained so until he acquired a lot of money, which he spent beyond his means. He was never middle class.

During my research on Fassbinder, I read that the original director of *Querelle* was to have been Werner Schroeter, but the producer couldn't raise the money for a project directed by him. At the time, this didn't mean much to me, because I had never seen a Schroeter film; they were almost impossible to see. A year or so later, I saw *The Death of Maria Malibran* and have never really recovered. The film, as critics say, defies description. It features Schroeter's regular star, the larger than life Magdalena Montezuma, as well as Warhol superstar Candy Darling (who appears as a boy on film for the only time). The soundtrack is a riot of clashing styles that somehow all coalesce into a harmonious whole, as in Jack Smith's *Flaming Creatures*. The images, with their inky blacks and glowing flesh tones, their tricks of perspective and focus, are unforgettable. The combination, I remember thinking when I first saw *Malibran*, creates a volatile and revolutionary cinema; it must have struck the spectators of 1971 (the year of its release) as the wave of the future. Unfortunately for Schroeter and his fans, this wave never crested.

Werner Schroeter's films were too queer, too aggressive in their experimentation, and too indifferent to the standards of naturalistic acting to impress film culture's gatekeepers with their seriousness. A competent pasticheur like Hans Jürgen Syberberg could take New York by storm with his immensely long and ponderous *Our Hitler*, but no one wanted to know about the director from whom Syberberg had stolen everything. Fassbinder, very much to his credit, decried this injustice and defended Schroeter in the German press, but it was too little too late (and in the wrong language) to persuade the Americans to accept a truly original body of work. Michel Foucault, astonished by *The Death of Maria Malibran*, also paid tribute: "What Schroeter does with a face, a cheekbone, the lips, the expression of the eyes, is a multiplying of the body, an exultation." I imagined a few well-placed cultural arbiters saying, "Who cares? It's just the homosexual cabal engaging in a little log rolling."

Despite my reservations, I decided to give *Querelle* another chance. I figured that if I didn't like the film, I might be entertained by the crowd that showed up. When I got to the theater, it wasn't the audience that interested me, but the new member of the staff. I discovered Al working there. I paid for my ticket and asked him how he was doing; from inside the ticket booth he said, "I'm the new box bitch" in his Cuban accent. There was a large line behind me so I didn't say anything in response.

Fassbinder's staging of the many variations of homosexual desire and self-loathing in *Querelle* caused me to reflect upon my relationship with Al, hardly a relationship at all, but something that occupied a larger space in my imagination than I would have wished. Al sought out doubles who looked exactly like him for sex; anyone else was just a fairy, the word the men in *Querelle* use to describe the undesirables. Al saw a weakness in me—my desire for him—and exploited it in a way that would humiliate me. I had always considered my throat to be my weak point; I regularly lost my voice, and I developed an aversion to fellatio. Al must have instinctively known that and exerted his dominance by raping my face. I should have been repelled by this aggression and avoided him from that moment onward, and yet I was drawn to him. I dearly wanted to fist Al. Perhaps that would cure me of my obsession with him, or at least enable me to turn the tables and change the dynamic between us. Had that ever been done to him? Or did his image of himself only admit to being a "total top"? I wanted to know what went on in his head, but I resigned myself to never knowing. Although I still couldn't say I enjoyed Fassbinder's *Querelle*, I realized that the film brought these thoughts to my mind more directly than any other film I had seen. I could barely stand to watch it, and if the uncomfortable laughs from the audience were any indication, many others felt the same way. I chose to leave for the men's room during the most excruciating moment of the film: Jeanne Moreau singing "Each Man Kills the Thing He Loves" in English.

On my way back from the urinals, I saw Al cleaning the concession counter. I was nervous, but I walked right up to him and blurted out a question: was he was still shooting pornos? He let out a sigh and said, "Not in a few years. Everything is shot on video now. I was shooting film for the companies, but they don't want that, too expensive. The reason they hire me, it's gone. So sad."

I said, "I loved porn when it was shot on film."

"Me too," he said. "But it's a different world now." Al went back to his task, signaling that he didn't want to continue the conversation. He might have been embarrassed to be seen doing work he considered beneath him, or maybe he just didn't like me all that much. I had hoped he would indulge me long enough to tell him a story. It related to *Querelle* in a way, and I was proud of it. I had rehearsed it like a routine over and over to myself, yet had never told another person. I felt wounded by Al's indifference, but I didn't let it hinder me. Since my intended audience didn't want to hear the story, I went home and wrote it down.

∞

I took the train from Cologne to Berlin, passing through the territory of the German Democratic Republic in the middle of the night. I arrived at Zoo Station at 6:15 in the morning, a time I had rarely seen from either direction, and it took all my effort to make my way to Rathaus Steglitz by U-bahn. I expected to see morning commuters, but I saw hardly any. I figured that was because I was going from the center to the suburbs, but actually words like "center" and "suburbs" had little meaning in West Berlin. The real center, Mitte, lay at the western edge of East Berlin. Surrounded by the wall, West Berlin was a forlorn, landlocked island in a city built for eight million but inhabited by less than half that number. There were forests and lakes inside the wall, and a few tall buildings, but mostly medium sized ones, like the one where I would be staying. I had a German-American friend, Martin, who wanted to live for a while in his father's country. If he took up residence anywhere in the Federal Republic of Germany, he would be conscripted into the army. Since West Berlin was not legally part of the Federal Republic, young men who lived there were exempt from the draft.

Martin, groggy and a little bit resentful, let me in and went right back to bed after showing me to my room. I lay down and slept past 10:30; when I got up, the place was deserted. Martin and his roommates had left for the day. I decided to visit Dahlem, where some of the art collections from Museum Island had been relocated after the war. The Dahlem Museums were a half hour away on foot, beyond the Botanical Garden. It was March and very cold in Berlin. I hoped the fresh air would wake me up.

Hardly anyone was in the Gemäldegalerie when I arrived. Alone and silent, I wandered from gallery to gallery looking at the art. I wanted to find Caravaggio's *Cupid Victorious*, the most salacious painting in a museum that prided itself on owning many Saint Sebastians. A printed museum guide pointed out that paintings of a nude man pierced by arrows were not understood as sexual at all when first exhibited, a thesis I thought impossible to defend beyond doubt.

On my way to Caravaggio, I heard some commotion from the only other visitors around. At a distance, I saw a man in a camel colored overcoat talking loudly to another man who was shorter and wore a black leather jacket. The taller man was speaking French, and it was obvious that he was gay. I approached a bit to eavesdrop. I saw that the taller man wore his hair in a ponytail and had a slightly worried expression on his face. He was trying to impress the other man but failing. His back was to me, but I could tell he was older, and he said almost nothing. The two were standing in front of a Breughel painting, but they argued about a Rembrandt, *The Man with the Golden Helmet*. At that time, the Gemäldegalerie (if not the entire city of West Berlin) used this painting as a promotional device; its popularity was second only to the famous one-eyed bust of Nefertiti in the Egyptian Museum. The old man stubbornly insisted that *The Man with the Golden Helmet* was not really by Rembrandt, but the younger man agreed with the traditional attribution and gave multiple reasons. (The old man was proven right within a year, and this painting by someone in the "circle of Rembrandt" fell into obscurity.) Finally, the old man said, *Tu as tort. Il n'y a rien à discuter*—you are wrong; there's nothing to discuss—and walked away.

I reached the gallery displaying *Cupid Victorious*, which was larger than I had expected. The nude figure in the painting is approximately life size. He thrusts his hairless genitals at the spectator, and the arrows in his right hand point at them for emphasis. He has the face not of a god, but of a boy who has had experience beyond his years. He tilts his head, and the look in his eye gives a wicked invitation. There is no malice in his gaze, only good humor and curiosity, yet the slight bags under his eyes suggest that he has made this proposition before. The title on the label was in Latin: *Amor Vincit Omnia*, love conquers all.

As I studied *Amor Vincit Omnia* carefully, I didn't notice that someone had come up behind me. I snapped out of my reverie and stepped aside. I turned towards the old man I had seen in the gallery earlier. I recognized his face: it was Jean Genet. He looked very frail, and his leather jacket completely enveloped him. He was pale and a little pink, and close-cropped white hair ringed his bald head. I could see his crooked nose, broken once many years before. I stared at him. When he was done looking at the painting, he turned to leave, and our eyes met. His gaze was warm and approving and a little mischievous. He had caught me staring, but was pleased to have upstaged a Caravaggio for a few seconds.

I later learned that this was the last year of Genet's life, and I imagined that he was making a tour of his favorite places while he was still able to do so. Genet had written about Rembrandt, and not counting *The Man with the Golden Helmet*, the museum owned twenty-five paintings by him. At the time, I wondered if Genet would one day write about Caravaggio; in the end, he didn't live long enough to do it. Unknown to everyone, he was at work on his last book, *Prisoner of Love*, and he let nothing distract him. Perhaps in the collection of the Gemäldegalerie he found the inspiration for describing a beautiful boy in the book, someone he had known in his youth, but whose features had faded from his memory.

In the brief instant I spent in Genet's presence, I didn't try to engage him in conversation. My French was poor, and I couldn't think of what to say. I don't regret not speaking to the old man. It was enough to exchange glances in a moment of complicity.

TEN

I continued to fist Raúl on a regular basis, but I knew our time together would end soon. I had gotten used to having a friendly partner, and I enjoyed my conversations with him. Meeting Raúl had changed me, and I began to want something more from the men with whom I had sex. I nearly stopped going to gay bars for which I had never felt much affection.

One evening, after I'd worked an early shift at the video store, I got a phone call from Anne.

"Hello, stranger. Where have you been?" she asked.

"Working a lot these days, I guess. I went to the New Beverly recently, and I saw you aren't the only box bitch anymore."

"Oh yeah, do you know that guy?" By that, Anne was asking if we had had sex.

"Barely. I know his cousin really well, we were friends at school, but Al has always given me the cold shoulder." There was absolutely no way I'd tell Anne about my feelings, such as they were, for her coworker.

"Hmm, you haven't been jonesing for any free food at the theater. You don't have a boyfriend or anything like that?" Anne could always tell when I wasn't being entirely truthful.

"Not exactly. He's going away to school in a few weeks. It's not that serious."

"You should come by the theater while I'm working some time. Unless you're one of those fags who cuts off all his friends when he gets laid regularly."

"I'm not. I'll see if Raúl wants to go to a movie."

"Yeah, do that." Anne sounded skeptical. She changed the subject. "Do you ever read the crime section of the *Los Feliz Ledger*?" I found this publication on my doorstep whenever the person delivering free newspapers noticed my apartment, which wasn't very often.

"I haven't seen it," I said.

She let out a throaty laugh. "There was a police report about a guy they found on Hyperion at three a. m. with his fist up his own ass. What the hell? Was he walking down the street like that?"

I laughed and said, "That doesn't seem possible, now does it?" For a second, I wondered if Anne somehow knew that I had been getting into fisting. I couldn't think of any way she could have known; perhaps she was just trying to draw me out on the subject.

"It's screwy. What's the LAPD up to anyway?" Anne sounded disappointed, but I couldn't tell if it was because she missed me, or because she wanted gossip and didn't hear any. "See you at the New Beverly."

"Okay," I said as she hung up.

∞

The last time Raúl and I saw each other before he went off to school was in early September. The heat and pollution in Los Angeles is usually at its worst in August, and when September comes, everyone gets excited at the prospect of relief, then let down when relief doesn't come until October or November. Many social rituals adhere to calendars imported from the East Coast, so the fall season for art exhibitions begins at a time when any sane person with money would be at the beach or holed up in air conditioned comfort. An exhibition of photographs by Joel-Peter Witkin had just opened at Fahey/Klein, and not wanting to experience the sweaty crush of the opening reception, I waited until the following weekend to see the show. I asked Raúl if he wanted to accompany me (and drive me there), and he said yes.

When we arrived, the gallery was as silent as a tomb. Spread out in neighborhoods all over the city, Los Angeles art galleries get very little foot traffic. Fahey/Klein, which was near a cement factory a couple of blocks south of the hustler strip on Santa Monica Boulevard in Hollywood, seemed to get virtually none; that's why I was surprised when Raúl saw someone he knew in the gallery. About fifteen minutes after us, another couple, a Latino man and an Armenian man, came in. The Armenian looked Raúl and me up and down, and took a quick stroll around the gallery. He told his boyfriend that he was going to Aron's Records on Highland, then to Los Tacos around the corner, where they could meet later.

Raúl introduced me to his friend Daniel, who looked like an ancient Olmec head placed on the body of a homeboy. He was bald and had prominent, sensual lips. His skin was brown, and his body was a bit round all over. He hid his extra weight with athletic clothes, a white tank top covered by a hooded sweatshirt and long basketball shorts. His boyfriend was dressed more or less the same way, and they wore roughly the same size, so I guessed they lived together and shared clothes. Daniel's interest in me was obvious from the second he walked in. I suspected the whole thing was a set up, that Raúl had suggested Daniel meet me, and John, the boyfriend, came along to approve the assignation. But I could tell that Daniel was interested in looking at the art, too.

The exhibition began with a warning about "adult content," always a good sign, and a number of the photographs in it were particularly memorable. The first had a complicated title, *Journeys of the Mask: The History of Commercial Photography in Juarez.* The square format print imitates the look of portraits of Storyville prostitutes by the New Orleans photographer E. J. Bellocq. A woman lies on a boldly striped Empire style divan. She stretches her torso so that her breasts do not protrude, giving her a somewhat androgynous look. Her eyes hide behind a blindfold with a crucifix attached. A riding crop rests across her neck. She wears a pair of black fishnet stockings and no other clothing. A dirty foot is visible above the divan. When I searched for the body attached to the foot, I found a man on his back with his legs in the air at the edge of the picture. Most of his body lies outside the frame, and only a pair of testicles indicates that this person is male. The reclining woman has thrust her right foot into the man's ass in a way that appears casual. At first glance, an inattentive viewer might not see that penetration figures in this picture at all, but once noticed, it becomes a focal point. The anonymity of the subjects, the dirty feet, the word "commercial" in the title—several things suggest that the photograph is a pornographic image, yet its composition is so clever, the scratches and faults in the emulsion are so obviously aesthetic, and the styling is so precise that the photograph could be nothing but art. I suppose this aspect of "looking like art" made the work a failure by my standards of the time, but in subsequent months, I was unable to forget it, and that counts for something.

The second photograph that caught my attention, *Arm Fuck*, drew an approving laugh from Daniel. I found the title puzzling, and I wondered if Witkin knew that the common term for the practice is "fist fuck." Perhaps the active partner in the scene was an amputee and had no fist, but that explanation seemed a bit convoluted. The photograph resembles the one representing a foot fuck: square and antique-looking, with the passive partner in exactly the same posture, on his back with legs in the air. One arm is also raised, suggesting the presence of a supporting sling that was removed by retouching. The active partner's face is a blur, indicating a long exposure. Most of the passive partner's body is visible, though his face is not; once again the person penetrated is anonymous. While I pondered this photograph, Daniel, who had wandered away for a bit, came up behind me. I could feel his breath on my neck, but I didn't move. He whispered in my ear, "I wish I could take an arm that deep." I shivered.

I turned to look at him and said, "I can help with that." He smiled eagerly. The sexual act performed in *Arm Fuck* was indeed one of the most impressive I had ever seen. The top's arm is buried in the bottom's ass almost all the way to the shoulder. I had suspected this was possible, and for the first time I saw the evidence of it right in front of me.

Daniel and I stayed together as we looked at the rest of the exhibition. Occasionally, he would make a comment like "I love dark stuff," or "I'll see these pictures in my dreams." I wanted to ask Daniel about himself, but I didn't think it was the right time or place. Raúl left us alone and killed time by looking at the checklist of works, biography, and catalogues that the gallery made available at the front desk. After a while, Raúl walked over, and the three of us looked at one of the more recent photographs in the show. *Feast of Fools*, made in New Mexico in 1990, rectangular in format and not as noticeably flawed as the earlier photographs—perhaps evidence that Witkin had abandoned certain aesthetic affectations— is a still life, or *vanitas*. A *vanitas* composition traditionally embodies the theme of life's brevity with symbols such as cut flowers (which always wilt) or fresh food (which always rots), and often, a human skull. *Feast of Fools* includes amputated human limbs and the cadaver of a baby, along with grapes, pomegranates, berries, shellfish, and an octopus. For some reason, Daniel shuddered at the sight of this picture and walked away. I looked at Raúl, but he gave no indication that he knew what was wrong. I found Daniel at the front desk, and I used one of the gallery's cards to write my phone number on the back. Daniel took it and said, "I have to get back to John," as he put the card in his pocket.

As we drove back to my place, I asked Raúl what he knew about Daniel. He told me that they had hooked up a few times but Daniel preferred white men, so their meetings were not a priority for him. Raúl said he wasn't angry at being slighted in this way, because Daniel was really crazy and could be difficult. He didn't explain what he meant, and I didn't ask him for details. I was interested enough in Daniel that I wanted to find out for myself.

Raúl asked me, "So who is this Witkin guy?"

I told him, "He became well known a few years ago with a photograph called *The Kiss*, which showed two halves of a cadaver's head kissing each other."

Raúl asked, "Where does he get cadavers?"

"He did *The Kiss* as a student at the University of New Mexico. The picture caused a scandal when some fundamentalist Christian administrator found out that Witkin had been using university resources to make art that the administrator personally felt was obscene. He banned Witkin from the university pathology labs and forced him to destroy the negative of *The Kiss*. For subsequent works, Witkin went to morgues in Mexico, where the rules were more lax and there was no moralistic reaction to his subject matter. I assume he also bribed people."

Raúl sighed and said, "No one does carnage like Latin America."

I continued, "That's an important point, because when Witkin started making these pictures, the situation in Central America was at its worst. I wouldn't go as far as saying that Witkin was literally illustrating political repression, but artists do have a way of expressing something in the air, in this case, the horrible violence that was taking place south of the border."

"What was the reaction to these pictures in the United States?"

I answered, "To Witkin's surprise, his work was politicized. Among conservatives, there was well-rehearsed shock and indignation, and among liberals, embarrassment. Senator Jesse Helms, that old windbag, denounced Witkin's work as an example of the 'moral corruption' of the National Endowment for the Arts. The US government, through the NEA, had given Witkin grants to make his photographs, and museums grants to mount exhibitions that included them. Witkin wasn't alone. Other photographers like Robert Mapplethorpe and Andrés Serrano were also attacked. It was dreadful, but at the same time amazing to read that Congressmen were asking questions about Mapplethorpe's photographs of fist fucking. Detailed descriptions ended up in the Congressional Record. There was a lot of self-righteous and ignorant posturing… well, ignorant about art, not about power politics. The ensuing moral panic caused the NEA to discontinue grants to individual artists."

Raúl said, "Well, that sucks."

"I think the whole sordid affair was a smoke screen. The controversy distracted from a real political issue: death squads in El Salvador committing atrocities with US support. Government expenditure on art is a tiny fraction of what is spent on the military. Even though it was not Witkin's explicit intention to criticize US foreign policy, I believe his work was ridiculed because it reminded politicians and their constituents of certain gruesome truths in Central America."

Raúl asked, "Did the general public know what was going on in El Salvador?"

I shrugged. "Some people did, but if you got your information mainly from television, you were probably just confused by it all. In the Reagan era, US Government officials invented their own narrative. It didn't matter if anything they said was true or not; in fact, it was better if it wasn't true. They could more easily twist things to their own advantage that way. This new frontier of bullshit, which we now have to deal with on a daily basis, is called perception management."

ELEVEN

After Raúl left for Chicago, Daniel called me, and we made arrangements to see each other a couple of days later. He explained that he needed twenty-four hours' notice before a fisting date so that he could control what he ate the day before. Cleaning out took three hours, and with travel time included, this meant Daniel would spend half a day having sex. Spontaneity, something I had heard about in pop songs and romantic comedies but hardly ever experienced, played little part in the rituals of fist fucking.

Shortly after I met Anne, she showed me something she had been reading, a case study of a compulsive fellator who sucked as many cocks as he possibly could in a tremendous variety of circumstances. When I considered all the preparation that went into fist fucking, I was jealous of this man and his kind. How gratifying it must be to know that at any time of day or night and in any location, some men are willing to drop their pants and get blown. If they can't get it up, no problem, the fellator will work to make them rock hard. And as long as no reciprocation is required, a man willing to be sucked off by a mouth belonging to another man can be serviced without ever raising the frightening and potentially messy prospect of anal sex. Utopia: any man can be had. Such a life was not for me. I craved other pleasures.

Daniel came to my apartment at the appointed hour carrying a backpack full of supplies: a towel, incontinence pads, two different kinds of lube (one thick and one thin, made from his own recipe), a couple of sex toys, poppers, a drinking bottle full of something that smelled alcoholic, and marijuana with a pipe and lighter. He asked me if he could smoke outside my door, and I said that would be fine.

After he took a hit of pot, he said, "Raúl told me you're very good."

"I hope so. He's the only guy I've ever fisted."

"I normally prefer old white men, because they have the most experience. I'm sure you'll do fine. By the way, I don't get fucked, only my boyfriend is allowed to go there. I can suck you off. Are you okay with that?" he asked.

"Sure. It was that way with Raúl, but he didn't have a boyfriend." I said.

"I'm hotter than he is." I gave Daniel a disapproving look, and he added, "or sluttier," and smiled broadly. "We can start as soon as the pot kicks in."

We went to my bed and undressed. Daniel sucked me off. He was very good at it, and when I was on the verge of coming, I forced his head down onto my cock. I could hear him choking a bit as I ejaculated down his throat. He came up for air after I was done and cleared his throat. All he said was "hot." I told him to get on all fours. "I like it better on my back," he protested.

"But I only know how to fist a bottom on all fours. I tried fisting Raúl on his back in a sling once, and it was like driving in England, everything was reversed. I want to make sure I don't hurt you."

"Okay," he said as he got into position.

I took the thicker lube and poured it over my right hand. I poked Daniel's asshole with my index finger. It wasn't like other holes I had known; there was less resistance, and it felt almost mushy. Before I knew it, I had four fingers inside him. I poured some of the thinner lube onto the area, and I worked my entire hand into Daniel's rectum. Daniel gasped a little and said "slower," but there was no need for concern. I found that if I turned my hand ninety degrees, his asshole opened up right away, like a key in a lock.

I began to draw my hand in and out, making regular movements, each thrust deeper by small increments. Daniel was moaning with pleasure. Once I had gone as deep as I thought I could, I stopped. I stretched my fingers a bit, and Daniel responded with a whine. I asked, "Are you okay?"

He managed to say one muffled syllable, "More."

I decided to try something new. From the depths of Daniel's ass, I took my hand out as quickly as I could with a jerk. Daniel screamed. This time, I didn't ask him how he was. He would have to submit to whatever I did to him. I had a feeling he preferred it that way.

I began pumping my hand in and out, from completely outside his ass to deep within it, in one fluid motion. I did this over and over until I felt Daniel get tense. Before his colon closed up tightly, I thrust my hand into his ass as deep as it would go. Daniel gasped. I wasn't concerned. I had seen no blood on my hand, and I figured if he was in serious pain, he would tell me. I left my hand inside him as his sphincter muscles tightened around it. Peristalsis comes in waves, so all I needed to do was to catch the next wave in a couple of minutes. I paused as his intestines caressed my hand.

As soon as Daniel's sphincters relaxed, I began to move again, stretching my fingers in a way that made me think of playing the piano. I turned my hand and Daniel let out a long, low moan. I started to make a fist, and the moan continued. Not moving backwards or forwards, I slowly drew my fingers up to the palm of my hand. I felt Daniel panic slightly, and his sphincter muscles contracted again. They became extremely tight around my fist. I said, "It's okay, you can do it." I waited a while, and finally, just as my hand was about to fall asleep, his colon opened wider than ever. It was my moment to pull out. In one continuous motion, smoothly but not quickly, I drew my fist out of Daniel's ass. He made a sound I had never heard before; it was more like someone giving birth than having sex.

I plunged my fist inside Daniel. There was much less resistance than I expected. I couldn't go as deep as before, because I hadn't unclenched my hand. I made this movement, in and out with a full fist, for quite a while. I was punch fisting for the first time. I wanted to see how deep he could take it, so I bore down on his insides with all my strength. I reached the place where I had first made a fist inside him, and I went a bit further. My entire hand and wrist, plus about half my forearm, fit inside. After a pause, I took a deep breath and pulled my fist out as quickly as possible. His entire body shuddered. I said nothing. He shuddered again. I knew not to touch or disturb him. He shuddered a third time. I remained there kneeling in front of him in silence as the waves of an intense orgasm shook his body. I looked at my hand. It was pink. There was no dark red blood. I had irritated his insides but not damaged them. I wiped off my hand with a paper towel as Daniel continued to experience the aftershocks of an orgasm.

Finally, Daniel got up from the bed and faced me. There were tears in his eyes. He cried as I watched him. He couldn't speak, but periodically he tried to form words. The crying went on for a long time. I had no idea how to respond. Should I attempt to hug him or keep my distance? Had I hurt him? Was he having a mental breakdown? I had never been this close to someone who cried without being able to stop. I checked his face for clues, but there were none. He continued to cry. I began to wonder if I should call an ambulance.

Daniel eventually pulled himself together and said, "That was beautiful. I've been fantasizing about this for years, and now I've found it."

∞

After our shower, Daniel collected the used pads from the bed, placed them in a plastic bag, and put the bag in his backpack, a gesture I appreciated. Once he was dressed and ready, he said, "I'm starving!"

"Let's go to Seafood Bay," I suggested.

We went to Sunset Junction in his truck, which was enormous. As a general rule, I associated large trucks with tiny penises. In Daniel's case, I wasn't sure, because I hadn't actually seen his penis. Only minutes after having sex with him, I could barely remember what his body looked like. How his insides felt and the sounds he made—those things I didn't forget—but the outside wrapping of it all was of less importance.

After we sat down and gave our orders, I asked Daniel, "Why did you cry so much today?"

"You don't know how good you are, do you?" I shook my head. "You broke me down and made me feel totally vulnerable. It was magic."

"Vulnerable how?"

"I work as a plant manager in a factory. I spend my days telling a bunch of Mexicans what to do. I have to be totally in control and masculine so they won't question my authority. When you fisted me, I was naked and scared, and I couldn't stop thinking what it would be like if all my employees saw me that way—the big, mean boss man reduced to a pathetic bottom bitch. It's totally humiliating." He was grinning when he said this.

"Are you into humiliation?" I asked.

"I like the feeling of being nothing but a hole, a thing without a cock. When I was naked, I noticed you never once looked at my crotch. That's the kind of humiliation I want."

"Good, because I'm not sucking you off."

Daniel looked overjoyed; whether it was because of what I said or because the food arrived at that moment, I didn't know. As we ate our fish, I asked Daniel about himself.

117

He said, "I was born in San Salvador, but I've been in the US for about ten years."

"You don't have an accent at all."

"Yeah, I'm totally whitewashed. Raúl wanted to speak Spanish with me when we played, but now my English is much better than my Spanish. I'm never going back to El Salvador."

I asked, "Where did you go to school?"

"Marshall High. I lived in your neighborhood when I was a teenager. Now I'm going to Cal State Northridge off and on, getting a degree in business, which I hate. But the goal is to be employable. Anyway, I like the Valley. My boyfriend and I are buying a house in Sylmar."

When we finished our food, Daniel asked for the check and paid. When I thanked him, he laughed. "I'm the one who should be thanking you."

∞

During the months that followed, I had the most intense sexual experiences of my life. It's a bit odd to describe them that way, because I felt very little physical sensation, aside from the relief of a few nice blowjobs. I was giving all the sensation to my partner. That might seem like a thankless task, but Daniel's capacity for taking whatever I could dish out was so great that I kept coming back for more. Every time I saw him, I was able to go deeper inside his body. I had seen a bend between the rectum and the colon in anatomical diagrams, and I expected that I would need to contort my hand a bit to get beyond it, as I had with Raúl. With Daniel, I didn't notice much resistance. He had figured out how to train his colon to relax and straighten out to accommodate large objects. From him I learned that my hands are not large but medium sized, and that the non-dominant hand is always slightly smaller than the dominant one, so when I wanted to try something new, it was usually possible with my left.

By the winter, Daniel was taking most of my forearm in his ass. I had gotten so deep inside him that I could feel the bend leading to his transverse colon with my fingertips. During our sessions, Daniel was insatiable, like a wild animal, and I was almost always the one to call an end to our play, either when my arms grew tired or when I began to notice a substantial amount of blood on my hands.

After we had known each other a few months, Daniel taught me a new trick. I would put my hand inside him until I couldn't go any deeper, and stay there. I would then back up to find the place where his pulse was the strongest. He'd take a big whiff of poppers and hold his breath for ten seconds. The moment he started to exhale, I vigorously massaged the spot. It always made him scream. An older gentleman in Palm Springs who had been getting fisted for decades taught Daniel this technique, the "E Ticket." He said the name came from the best pass at Disneyland, the one giving access to the entire park, called the "E Ticket" in the 1970s. When done correctly, it would feel like riding on Space Mountain times a thousand or being shot directly to the stars. All Daniel could say about the experience was that it felt like heaven.

At the best moments of our sessions, Daniel remained silent. He told me that while experiencing intense sensations, he sometimes saw a mental image of a landscape. He pictured himself at the top of a cliff looking down on beautiful green fields. I asked if he recognized the place, and he said no. As far as he could tell, it came from his imagination.

∞

What kept me interested in Daniel was not only the desire to see how much he could tolerate, but a curiosity about his personality.

I never asked his age, but I assumed he was no older than his mid-twenties, and I was astounded by a level of perversion that I had previously associated only with senior citizens and characters in Sade novels. His imaginative capacity was immense, and every time I spoke to him, there would be some new fantasy he'd share. He was particularly drawn to horses, and the idea of being fucked by a stallion, or fellating one, obsessed him. He talked about finding access to horse semen and using it as a lubricant for sex. I asked him why horses were so important in his fantasy life, and he said, "They just want to fuck. If a horse mounts you, you can't say, 'Stop, I need a break,' because it doesn't understand. It's a beast. To take a horse cock, you have no choice but to relax. If you don't, you could get killed." He added, "I think about a horse cock sometimes when your fist is deep inside me, and it helps me to open up." My reaction to Daniel telling me this was like the reaction most people have to a photograph of a puppy: isn't that cute? His stories warmed my heart.

Daniel's relationship with his boyfriend seemed more or less normal, which is to say a sexual partnership that settled into something more like an intimate friendship after a couple of years. John and Daniel had an extremely open relationship, and that suited John, since he was a major slut himself, though as far as I could tell, vanilla by Daniel's standards. I wasn't very nosy, but I did once ask Daniel about how things were going with his boyfriend.

"I can sum that up in two words: no sex. But it's okay. We like different things now."

I asked, "What does he like?"

"John likes to fuck and be done with it, get his dick sucked and show no regard for the other guy's needs. He has tons of regulars, guys lining up to suck him off. One of the things he's proudest of is how thick his dick is. When he realized I'm getting fists inside me, it killed that whole 'I'm gonna tear up your ass with my cock' thing. He can't compete with an arm, which is why he lost interest."

Daniel described John as "masculine and entitled," traits that were very attractive to him. Their relationship had gotten serious very quickly, and John started bringing Daniel to family gatherings within a couple weeks of meeting him. He was not entirely out of the closet to his large Armenian family, so the presence of a Salvadoran boyfriend at three-day long wedding ceremonies and huge celebratory banquets caused a stir. He didn't care.

The most challenging part of the relationship was John's devotion to Madonna. Daniel called her "that witch." For the sake of household peace, he was obliged to smile and make nice whenever Madonna released a new record, or worse, starred in a movie. During the concert tours, John would insist on spending thousands of dollars to see his idol's live shows, and Daniel would have to go along (as well as pay for his own ticket). The only subversive pleasure Daniel took was in watching the movie *What Ever Happened to Baby Jane?* repeatedly, imagining that the story of a washed-up child star of silent films living in a fantasy world and looking like a painted ghoul was a premonition of Madonna's future. John never suspected a thing.

∞

Somewhat to my surprise, I discovered that Daniel preferred Joan Crawford to Bette Davis. I had always thought Joan's acting was a little insipid, while I found Bette endlessly entertaining to watch. With this in mind, I invited Daniel out on a date of sorts, to a screening of *What Ever Happened to Baby Jane?* at the New Beverly. I figured if Daniel could put up with Madonna, I could certainly compromise on Joan Crawford, who had made some great films. We went to the theater on a night Anne was working at the ticket booth. She let us in for free.

"Long time no see." Anne made a wounded face. She looked Daniel up and down and asked, "Is this your boyfriend?"

"Not exactly."

Anne drew her head back a little and gave me a skeptical look. "You said the same thing about your last boyfriend."

"I'll talk to you later. I've seen *Baby Jane* many times, and I'm sure I can take a break." We let Anne get back to selling tickets and passed through the lobby.

Daniel and I found seats near an aisle, and the film began to the approving hoots of an almost entirely gay audience. After about twenty minutes, the crowd settled down. I was thinking about when it would be the best time to leave and talk to Anne. Then I looked over at Daniel, and I noticed tears in his eyes. I asked, "Are you okay?"

He said, "They just threw her away."

"Who?"

"The studios. When she was young and beautiful, she was in so many movies, and when she got older, no one wanted anything to do with her."

"Bette?" I asked without thinking.

"No, Joan. I love her," Daniel said as tears rolled down his cheek. I held his hand.

I excused myself to take a bathroom break close to the film's ending, which I had never thought was very satisfactory. I found Anne behind the concession counter after I returned from the men's room. She asked, "Time for your din din, Blanche?"

I laughed. "No, I already ate with Daniel."

"He seems nice."

I said, "Yeah, but he already has a boyfriend he lives with."

"Hmm, no future in that." Anne was distracted by arranging the candy in its glass case.

"No future, but the present has been… pretty amazing. He's about the most perverted person I've ever met in my life."

Anne gave me a vague look of distaste, which I didn't expect. In years past, she reveled in stories of sexual perversions, but now when it came to a friend's sex life, she was squeamish. I wondered what had changed. I asked her how she was doing, and she told me that this was her last week at the New Beverly. She had found a job at a graphic design firm with an office downtown. She was relieved to be making a decent wage and hoped to buy a better car. I noticed that her appearance had softened a bit, perhaps in preparation for more conventional employment. Her nails, which had previously been filed to sharp points, the better to defend herself against men or to scratch them during sex, had been given a more or less regular manicure and were painted a beautiful black with a reddish cast. I said, "Nice nails," wished her luck with her new job, and went back into the theater in time to see Bette Davis dancing in the sand.

∞

One day, after a particularly intense fisting session, Daniel told me something out of the blue. "You know, you remind me of my stepdad."

I asked, "What should I make of that?"

Daniel got the sort of look in his eye he did when he talked about sexual fantasies. "My stepdad used to beat me."

"That's terrible," I said, not knowing what else to say.

Daniel continued, telling me that his stepfather used to punish his sister and him by making them stand on tip toes with their knees bent, arms outstretched and books piled on top of them. They had to stay in that position for hours until they were crying from pain, while their stepfather casually watched a *telenovela*. Daniel said he thought getting his ass punched took him back to that pain, but on his own terms now.

I asked the first question that came into my head, "Did you ever see your stepfather naked?"

"No, but I knew he had a massive crotch. He was horse hung."

I asked, "Did your mom know he abused you?"

He hesitated. "Yes… but no. She didn't do anything about it until we were older. Before that she had to be quiet. When my mom first came to the US, she was working in a sweatshop. She was so poor she could barely eat. When this man promised to help her bring her kids to the States, she married him. I'm sure his horse cock was part of it. He was savage with my sister, because she wanted that cock. He used to beat her with a leather belt. Me, too. One time he was punishing me, arms up knees bent, and I prayed to God if he let me stop suffering I would go and kiss his feet. When he set me free I went to remove his shoes and he kicked me away. I was so humiliated."

I asked, "Was your stepfather queer?"

"I think he had tendencies. He used to work at a gay bar as a dishwasher when he first arrived from El Salvador. When I came out, he told me that he once almost went home with a guy."

"Almost." I laughed. For a brief instant, Daniel glared at me, and I stopped.

He said, "I hate my stepdad. But today, while you were fisting me, I realized that I'm in love with him. So I'm confused."

I said, "Sorry to remind you of him."

"Don't apologize. I'm not really hurt by it. It's fascinating to me. I'm more curious about why I like what I like and how it's all connected." I said nothing, hoping he would continue. "I'm a dirty pig. One day I want to get bred by a horse. I want my hole to be so wide that a guy can fuck me without feeling my ass lips around his cock at all. My asshole should look like the crater of a volcano." I nodded and smiled. "I want to be handcuffed and sitting at a wooden table with my nipples right above the surface. Then I want a masked man to come in with a hammer and nails. He gives me a massive whiff of poppers and pulls out my nipples and nails them to the table."

After a pause I asked, "Your boyfriend doesn't know any of this, does he?"

He said, "No man, only you. I like telling you my crazy thoughts. That's the kind of shit you like to hear, isn't it?"

I replied, "I'm the father confessor… or maybe in your case, the stepfather confessor."

Daniel snapped out of his state and brought up our next date. "See you Sunday? I'm yours whenever you want. John is out of town."

I asked, "When does he return?"

"In ten days. He's gone next weekend, too. So you're going to be punching me a lot." He paused. "What do you want it to look like when you're done?"

"Your ass?" I asked, and Daniel nodded. I made up something that would please him. "Raw hamburger stuffed down a big deep hole."

He smiled. "Fantastic. I want my hole to stop functioning, just to hang there useless, like a pair of big, droopy lips."

"Like in *Citizen Kane*." I said in a hoarse whisper, "Rosebud."

Daniel looked very serious. "Absolutely. Will you help me?"

I said, "I am the architect of your destruction."

TWELVE

Raúl came home to Los Angeles for the summer, and I could hardly believe that nine months had passed since I'd last seen him. We met at a Thai restaurant in East Hollywood. I had hoped we might have sex, but he said nothing about getting fisted. I think he preferred to be just friends. This made me wonder if he had started a serious relationship, but I didn't inquire about it.

He asked me, "Have you enjoyed fisting Daniel?"

I laughed. "You get right to the point don't you? He's a trip."

"I tried to warn you."

I smiled, "I know, he has his moments, but it's okay. He's an incredible pig." I changed the subject. "How are things in the anthropology department?"

A serious look came over Raúl's face. "Uh… could be better. It's been tough."

"Why?"

Raúl explained, "Dealing with the university isn't easy. I have to assert myself every step of the way. My work was questioned because it was supposedly too good for an immigrant. I started hearing about this drama of someone who's applying for a grant, that this person might not get it because some people were suspicious that the work submitted was plagiarized. I was thinking, 'Oh my God, this is so absurd.' Then I realized they were talking about me. I was like, 'Holy shit, we need to clarify this.' Of course, some people were very helpful about it, saying, 'No. This is the quality of work he's been submitting. This is not one of those cases.' But there was skepticism at the same time. 'You were not born here. How can you produce this kind of work?' Umm, smart people come from all over the world. Why do I have to keep proving myself so I can have access to the same resources that any other student has?"

He continued, "You have this group of scholars who are very invested in keeping scholarly work centered on a particular narrative of straight, white maleness. I feel dirty saying that, but the point is, it's a real thing. It still happens in academia—if you don't fall into all three of those categories, then you will be questioned no matter what."

"Are they accusing you of special pleading?" I asked.

"They never accuse me openly, but a bunch of people did backhandedly allude to that: 'Oh, it's just affirmative action,' In one of my early classes, the professor said, 'You are using this particular framework, and you're using examples from your native culture. I don't have knowledge about this, so I can't grade you.' I had to tell him, 'Well, how is that my problem? You're the professor. Use your methodology. Grade me on that.' I think the most insulting thing for him was that I introduced something new. Since he couldn't handle it appropriately, I wasn't supposed to bring it up. It's difficult for academics to admit that they don't know something. They're supposed to have a command of their field, but if you draw the boundaries of the field in a different way, suddenly they don't know anything. They're not in the center anymore, and they're thrown into crisis when their work is no longer relevant." Raúl sighed. "You know what else happened to me? They wanted to put my work under the label of Chicano Studies. I said, 'I'm not Mexican, nor am I of Mexican descent. That doesn't work.'"

"Oh, Chicago… How's your social life?"

Raúl looked serious again. "Well, social interaction has been a little awkward because my family's not upper middle class. Students really prioritize interaction based on how much access you have to wealth. To me, it's weird. People at first seem very nice, you'll have a relationship with them, and then all of a sudden it hits them, 'Oh, what do you mean you're a poor immigrant?' Then they'd kind of zone out. They have no way of understanding that reality. They basically dress like models right out of catalogue pages. Everyone else who is doing doctoral work also has a job. There are these enclaves of people who would get together and just say, 'Well, let the rich kids do whatever they want, and we'll do whatever we want.' It was a very clear divide of where you hung out and who you hung out with. In Latin America, I saw a little bit of that, but at the end of the day we could still share spaces and relationships with people who were wealthier than us. Here, wealth makes a bigger difference."

I asked, "Have you made friends with any of the rich kids?"

"This semester, I met a *fresa*…"

I looked surprised. "A strawberry?"

"It's a slang term. A preppy kid from a wealthy family in Mexico City is called a *fresa*. Strawberries are delicate and require the labor of a lot of poor workers to raise them. They can be delicious, but they may not be worth the effort."

"Ah, I see!"

He said, "On the level of discourse, we had a lot of things in common. At least it seemed like that. He was one of the few Latin American people who was willing to speak Spanish with me. That was a big thing, because I don't get to practice my Spanish very often in Chicago. Besides the fact that he was handsome. I think that's what kept it going a little longer than it would have otherwise.

"Anyway, he comes from an upper middle class family. He isn't super-rich. The richest kids in Mexico don't bother to study, because they are handed everything they could ever want no matter what they do. This guy has something to prove, he wants to be part of the ruling elite in a system that's completely rotten with corruption. I said to him, 'That's not me at all. I'm poor. Is that going to be an issue?' He said, 'No, it doesn't have to be an issue.' We hooked up a couple of times. He's versatile, which is nice. We fisted each other. The problems started when we had real conversations. I couldn't believe the shit that came out of his mouth. I asked him, 'How can you be so conservative?' Then I thought, why am I even asking this question? He comes from a well off Mexican family, he has political ambitions, and he studies economics in Chicago." He paused. "The most amazing thing is that he's a fan of Augusto Pinochet."

I was startled. "You can't be serious."

"Oh my God, when we had that conversation I thought, 'You know what? Maybe we can't be friends.' His defense was, 'He's a guy who knew what he was doing.' I said, 'Did he really? I understand you're from Mexico, but the negative impact he had on South America was huge.' He just idolized the guy. I couldn't let it drop when he said, 'but he had some redeeming qualities.' I had to ask, 'What are these redeeming qualities? I would love to at least understand where you're coming from.' Then he kept talking about power and military cunning and stuff like that. Then I told him, 'You get a boner for dictators. It doesn't have to be Pinochet. You just want a fascist daddy to dominate and fist you. That's your thing, clearly.' He got very offended."

"Does this guy work for the CIA?" I asked, half joking.

Raúl nodded. "That came up one day. His whole deal was, 'Oh, I wish I could, but I don't know if I'm good enough.' I couldn't believe he's still bowing down to the sense of 'I'm not good enough for the US Government.' He would've worked for the CIA, absolutely, in a second. That was one of his aspirations."

I rolled my eyes. "Your *fresa* has latched onto the only success in the history of the CIA, as far as anyone outside the agency knows. Almost every other project they undertook was a failure due to their total incompetence. Ivy League idiots! They couldn't kill Fidel Castro in Cuba, but they managed to kill Salvador Allende and install Pinochet in Chile." I paused and fantasized for a moment about fisting a handsome young fascist. "Hmm… maybe I can see the attraction of that guy."

Raúl interrupted my reveries. "Well, it's not happening anymore. I can't talk to him." He suddenly looked very angry. "Our last conversation was about politics, and things got pretty tense. As a 'fuck you' to me, he brought up Shining Path. He said they were an example of leftists really messing things up, and that I, as a Peruvian, couldn't possibly take them seriously. He mentioned their recent actions—kidnappings, sabotaging the infrastructure, car bombs—which everyone agrees are horrible, but he conveniently forgot about the poverty and oppression that made Shining Path come to prominence in the first place. I left Peru years ago, but my relatives there say it's dangerous even to bring up Shining Path in conversation now. I wanted to tell this guy that an uncle of mine is in prison for 'subversion by Marxist indoctrination.' He was a teacher whose students were very poor. He wanted to help them. He wasn't blowing things up. Anyway, I was so mad that this little piece of shit was trying to provoke me with stuff he knew nothing about that instead of arguing with him, I just turned and walked away. I haven't spoken to him since."

"It's good you didn't tell him anything personal. You could end up in some CIA dossier."

He said, "Believe me, I know." He shook his head and changed the subject. "So that's not the big news. Guess what? My dad came out."

I couldn't believe it. "What? Your father is gay?"

Raúl said, "Yeah, I had suspected something for a while. It started in the weeks before Christmas last year. He would just disappear for hours during the day, and my mom would say, 'I wonder where your dad is,' and it turned out he was getting rammed at some bathhouse. I remember when I was growing up, he used to go regularly to a Turkish bath in Lima. People thought this was so exotic. As an adult, now I say, 'Oh, that makes a lot of sense. He's a dirty little bitch.'

"The closer my relationship with my mom became, the more I realized that my parents were just friends. I wouldn't say roommates, because I do believe that there's an element of romantic love in their relationship, or maybe that's what I'm seeing because I'm their son. I didn't know it wasn't normal for couples to sleep in separate beds until I was a teenager, for example. They'd done that throughout their whole marriage. When I saw my dad not embodying the typical Latin *macho*, at first I thought, 'He's just very open-minded.' Then I realized this was his queerness coming through, but he's not allowing himself to embrace it."

I said, "Poor guy. He's a fifty year-old man who's just coming out now. He must be so frustrated… and jealous."

"Yes. Me and my dad, we have some friends in common. They told me, 'Your dad doesn't hate you, but he's upset because you can do what he could never dream of doing.'"

"Because he grew up in Peru?" I asked.

"Because he didn't allow himself to, not just because he was in Peru. It was my grandma, one hundred per cent. Grandma on my dad's side, she's a raging religious bitch. If she was my mother instead of my grandma, I don't think I could have come out either, just because that's how much of a presence she can be once she grabs hold of you."

"So it has to do with religion." I said.

Raúl explained, "It's partially religion, but for him, it was more about the social performance of someone who's a pastor, a father, a husband to a woman. It never occurred to him that there are mixed orientation marriages. When I brought it up, it blew his mind. He was like, 'People make it work?' I said, 'Yes, but in order for it to work, you have to be honest with one another, and you have to be honest with yourself.' I don't think my dad is there yet. Whatever he's into, I support him, unless it's an abusive relationship, which tends to happen with older Latin American men. I also said, 'Dad, I understand. You need to get something out of your system, but going to a bathhouse for eleven hours, maybe it's not the best way to go about it.'"

As he did every time I saw him, Raúl looked at his watch, made his apologies, and after dropping me off, went back to his family drama.

∞

In the days following my lunch with Raúl, our conversation disturbed me more and more. I had never devised any specific plans for my future after college, but vague notions of having a relationship and continuing my education reassured me. I could start a life with someone, I used to think, but now the most interesting available person I'd met in Los Angeles had moved out of state and was probably involved with someone else. I hadn't asked Raúl about it because I didn't want to hear his answer.

Even worse for me to hear was Raúl's account of his life in Chicago. In my mind, getting a master's degree—I couldn't imagine going as far as a doctorate—was an escape from the drudgery of the workplace, and maybe, if I was lucky, the beginning of a career (an ugly word that described a thing I wish I had). Although I was not a poor immigrant, Raúl's demoralizing (and expensive) experiences in academia did not inspire me with much hope for graduate school.

From my earliest youth, I had problems with authority, and they continued to manifest themselves during my undergraduate education. In college I had been trained to respect the Western canon, and when confronted with these great works, I was intimidated into silence. All of my professors asked the implied question, how can anyone rival the grandeur of these masterpieces? It felt pointless to write anything in their wake, but at the same time, what I read struck me as inadequate and out of date. In these texts I saw little that I understood as relevant to my own life. This is a trivial objection, an authority figure would say in response, and I would fly into an inarticulate rage. As a consequence, I developed a revulsion to grand totalizing statements and monuments of any kind. The ambition to encompass the spirit of an age in a single work struck me as idiotic and corrupt. The giant works of art taking up space in museums held no appeal, and the massive volumes that dilettantes snapped up in bookstores seemed as heavy as cinder blocks and just about as interesting. I suppose I had a lot in common with the Futurists, without (I hoped) their latent fascism. Any "universal" culture rang false to me because it was irredeemably compromised by the egotism and smugness of artists and the blood-soaked history they memorialized.

I felt paralyzed by my education, and I remained silent for years. Eventually, out of a simple desire to express myself, I started to write again. Tentatively at first, I wrote about my own experiences in a voice that didn't embarrass me. I knew I had no ability to make a grand statement, but I also knew I had something to say.

The final element that fell into place was the sexual adventure I had begun with my friends. As I started fisting, I wanted to describe it. I imagined an academic or commercial environment rejecting what I wrote as pornography, yet I was compelled to write these unwelcome texts in my own way and on my own terms. I wrote in longhand—I had never learned to type properly—and it occurred to me that in doing this I was liberating my hand. The movements of manipulating a pen were not so different from what I did to manipulate a man's innards. One activity made the other possible.

THIRTEEN

By the late fall, I had set aside enough money from working at the video store to buy a plane ticket, and I decided to visit my mother and spend Christmas with her. It would be the first time I'd seen her since I left for California more than two years before. She was overjoyed, and I had hopes for the trip myself. Perhaps I would be able to find a way to talk to her about something other than my father or her political activities. Regarding her politics, I could at least say that I no longer held a grudge against my mother's companions at the office. If anything, I was thankful to them, because they had kept her company after my father's death and given a structure to her days.

The conservative politics of resentment suited my mother perfectly. She felt she deserved better from life, and although she would never say so, her only reason for thinking this was that she was white. She had not been born into a position of privilege, and her efforts to rise in the world had not been rewarded as she hoped. It was her misfortune to have spent her entire life in a crumbling ruin of a city. She had grievances, many of them completely legitimate and understandable. So did I. But the objects of her scorn were different from mine. Consequently, we had nothing much to say to each other.

When state socialism collapsed in Eastern Europe, I wondered what would happen to my mother's world view. The great Satan, communism, was no longer the threat it used to be, so another adversary was needed to stir the American masses into a patriotic frenzy. When I asked her who the new enemy would be, my mother replied calmly, "The Third World."

My mother had gotten married when she was young, and she knew little about anything beyond her immediate ken. My father, who was older, had been more worldly, and I suspect he was a great pervert, too, if a repressed one. Why else would he have become such a big drunk? My mother loved my father, but I don't believe she understood him. And if my father was a mystery to her, I held out little hope that she could understand me.

∞

When I arrived at the small regional airport that served my hometown late one winter night, it was deserted. There were few flights available, and with a connection, it took a whole day to get there from the West Coast. Most of my fellow passengers were military personnel on their way home to see family. They had found their way out of town, too.

On the drive to my mother's house, a deer crossed our path. She said she'd seen quite a few of them lately. With little traffic on the roads, they felt bold, and the danger of hitting one with a car was great, as it is in the country. I had never considered the place where I grew up "the country," but nature had begun to reclaim large parts of what was once an industrial landscape. Perhaps after the last of my mother's generation dies, I thought, wildlife will take over the place. This may seem far-fetched, but it happened on a small scale in my own family.

My mother's sister Louise inherited a house from her mother-in-law, and she was unwilling or unable to sell it for decades. After aunt Louise's death, the abandoned house was opened so the heirs could see if anything remaining could be salvaged. Inside the house, tall weed trees had grown and layers of leaves and excrement littered the floors. Rats, raccoons, and deer had been living for a while in this interior forest. The house had suffered so much damage that demolishing it was the only solution. When we drove past the place, I noticed that the vacant lot where it once stood was still for sale.

My mother and I exhausted our habitual topics of conversation fairly soon, and I ran out of things to do to help her around the house. Not long after I arrived, a snowstorm hit, and for a couple of days, we were snowed in. I had forgotten what that was like; if I had remembered, I would have thought twice before booking a flight in December. I could spend a week at a time barely leaving my apartment in Los Angeles, because I knew I could go out at any moment I chose, but when I was trapped in my childhood home during winter, cabin fever set in quickly.

My mother had recently subscribed to cable television and the novelty had not yet worn off. She constantly switched from channel to channel as she watched. She was a bit hard of hearing, and the sound of the television was so loud that it was impossible to escape. She had a tendency to doze off while watching, and during her little naps, I would attempt to turn down the volume, which would often as not have the effect of waking her up. I found all of this particularly frustrating because I had resolved to work on my writing while I was visiting her.

In close proximity to my mother and with that racket interrupting my thoughts, I remembered a writer Moira had told me about, Osvaldo Lamborghini, a neo-Baroque Argentine modernist, supposed ladies' man, and probable sodomist. Upon returning from an extended trip to Spain during the early 1980s, he avoided Buenos Aires at the behest of concerned friends who wished to prevent him from being imprisoned or murdered by the ruling military dictatorship. Stranded in provincial exile at the family home in Mar del Plata, surrounded by relatives watching soccer with the television blaring, Lamborghini methodically wrote *Las hijas de Hegel* in his refined, complex prose full of allusions and wordplay, without crossing anything out or rewriting, before keeling over from a heart attack in 1985.

I could hardly imagine achieving such a state of concentration, so I decided instead to compete with the sound coming from my mother's television. I hauled her electric typewriter out of the basement. It was a great metallic lump of a thing, obsolete but in good enough shape to produce a decent manuscript. I started banging out my text as best I could, revising as I typed, and somehow at the end of the second snowbound day, I finished my text. The result was forty pages, double spaced. I remembered that I had Daniel's information in my address book. I wanted him to read what he had inspired. I would make a photocopy of the manuscript and mail it to him.

The next day, I drove my mother to Republican headquarters in the morning. She let me borrow her car while she was at work, as long as I picked her up afterward. I thought it unwise to use the party's photocopy machine, so I went to a copy store to prepare my package for Daniel. I included a handwritten note with my mother's phone number, and I mailed it from the downtown post office. After that, I drove around the area to pass the time. I had bought cassettes to play in the car on these road trips. The selection at the local stores was so poor that I was forced to buy a lot of classic rock, exactly the same music I heard on the radio and hated when I was an adolescent. The retro soundtrack, gray skies, and ruined landscape covered with dirty snow combined to sinister effect. Mantras played repeatedly in my head: "You have never really left"—"You are doomed to failure"—"All effort is futile."

∞

A phone call came to the house that night. I answered it in my old bedroom.

A woman's voice said, "Hello, do you know who this is?"

"Moira? I was just thinking of you today."

"I didn't expect to reach you. I was going to ask your mother for your phone number in LA."

Moira sounded not quite herself, as though she was suffering from exhaustion or some illness. I asked, "Are you okay?"

"I'm just tired is all. I've been working hard."

"What are you doing?"

"Organizing." Her voice was hoarse. I imagined I was one of hundreds of people to whom she spoke that day.

"I thought you went abroad."

"I did." There was a long pause, then she said, "I ended up going to El Salvador. It was horrible. I saw things no one should have to see. Somehow people cope with this on a daily basis. Life there has become all about death. I once saw a group of kids playing soccer with a decapitated head." There was another pause. "Psychos with automatic weapons are running rampant. No one is safe. And it's all being done with the support of the US Government. Your tax dollars at work. Our country is run by a bunch of genocidal lunatics, as it's always been. Don't let anyone tell you different. I used to think that the US might one day be involved with things that rival Nazi atrocities. Now I know it's already happening." With a tone of complete contempt, she spat out the words, "What they call democracy is a complete sham."

The Moira I remembered was back. I very much wanted to talk with her, but I wasn't eager to hear about mass murder just before bedtime. I changed the subject. "Are you in the United States now?"

She said, "I am. In the belly of the beast."

I asked, "Have you been in touch with your family?"

"Yeah, about that, you gave my dad the impression I'm a terrorist or something. Thanks a lot." Her sarcasm stung me.

"I said no such thing. He jumped to conclusions. I wanted to reassure him that you were safe, even though I knew nothing about your situation. I guess I messed up. I'm sorry." I was annoyed. It wasn't my fault that her parents worried when she didn't contact them for long periods. I asked, "What's this call really about?"

"I wanted to let you know…" There was a catch in her voice, and I heard her start to cry. "Al is dead. He had AIDS."

I was stunned. "I am so sorry." I didn't know what else to say.

"He was completely in denial and didn't get treatment… or else he knew he was infected all along, and he just didn't bother. Those meds are toxic. Anyway, it was very sudden."

"I saw him a while ago and he seemed fine." As I said this, I realized that a year and a half had passed since then. I asked, "How is your family taking it?"

"Not well. Most of my relatives pretend they knew nothing about his sexuality, but he was a *marielito*, and he wasn't a murderer or thief. What did they think? Fortunately, no one in the family has taken the position that he suffered God's judgment."

"Ugh," I said. "It's so sad. I always liked Al."

"I know." She asked, "Did you ever have sex with him?"

"Not exactly." I didn't know how to explain what happened between us. The news of Al's death gave the episode in the Blacklite rest room a new meaning, one I didn't want to dwell upon.

She said, "You'd better get tested. At least they can do that now."

"I have been tested, and the results were negative."

"You'd better play safe from now on," she said adamantly.

I told her, "I have the safest sex I can." Strictly speaking, this was a lie, but I didn't feel up to justifying myself to Moira. "Actually, I've been fist fucking." At that moment my mother came into the room. Since my father's death, she had become accustomed to a silent house, and the conversation must have roused her from a deep sleep. Perhaps she had some kind of maternal sixth sense that alerted her when talk about radical politics and fist fucking invaded her home. "Hey Moira, I should go. It's late here, and I just woke up my mother. Do you have a number where I can reach you?"

"No, I'm moving soon. I'll call you."

Somehow I knew she wouldn't. I gave her my phone number in Los Angeles anyway and said, "My condolences about Al, and thanks for letting me know. Take care of yourself."

"I will, Guillermito. Bye."

∞

A few days later, another phone call came at around ten p. m. It was Daniel. He sounded upset.

"What's wrong?" I asked, even though I knew more or less what he was going to say.

"I read your story." Daniel inhaled then exhaled. "We need to talk."

I tried to explain, "I thought what we've done has been so amazing that I had to write about it."

"Yeah, it *is* amazing, but it's private. I liked what you wrote, but I threw it away, because I don't want John to find it." He paused. "Are you planning to publish this?"

I hadn't given much thought to the question, but I said, "Maybe. Why not?"

"Do you want to ruin my relationship? We'd lose this house if we don't live together. I'd have to find another job, because we work together, too." He had rehearsed a litany of disasters in his head and was unleashing it on me.

"I doubt anyone you know would read this text if it were published." I believed this to be true, but it came across as snobbish and only made Daniel angrier.

He exploded, "This isn't about what people read or don't, it's about respect! Don't publish it."

I felt like exploding in response. Daniel saying the phrase "it's about respect," which sounded like a line from a movie, made me not want to concede anything, even though I had no immediate plan to publish the text. In my anger, an image involuntarily came into my mind. I saw a spread in the *New Yorker*—complete with smugly saccharine cartoons, the word "coöperate" spelled with a dieresis, and ads for upscale merchandise—devoted to the magazine's first publication of a story about fist-fucking, a term I imagined the editor would hyphenate. It was as unrealistic a fantasy as I had ever entertained, but for the rest of the conversation I couldn't stop thinking about it. I became intransigent. "You're not going to tell me what I can and can't write. I take this seriously."

"And you think I don't?" Daniel was shouting. "You didn't even change our names!"

"Well, that I can do," I said with a tone of unctuous patience calculated to drive Daniel crazy.

He took another breath and said calmly, "Listen, it's the story or me. Do you care more about a piece of writing or what we have?"

Given that ultimatum, there was only one way I could respond. The question became clear to me: Should I suppress my work for the sake of an affair with a man with a boyfriend? I said, "I'm sorry, I can't choose you over my writing."

"Okay, bye." And with that, Daniel hung up on me.

∞

I told my mother, who had been awakened by Daniel's call, that I needed to borrow her car to see a friend, an obvious lie. I didn't have any friends in the area, never had. My mother didn't question me. I left for a gay bar in the neighboring city. It had a wonderfully tasteless name: Booby's Why Not? Club. Why not, indeed. It was a longer drive than I expected, and I had time to think about my argument with Daniel. I remembered my high school composition class and the assignment I was forced to rewrite. My sense of logic told me the man I was fisting had nothing to do with that patriotic prick of a writing teacher, but Daniel's demand triggered something in me, a visceral hatred of censorship in any form. That someone would attempt to exercise control over a piece of my writing, even one with a readership of two people, made me simmer with rage. I still felt remorse for acquiescing to a teacher's authority. I remembered a lecture I had heard in college. A visiting professor presented short art films made during the Third Reich, productions that theoretically offered their directors more freedom than Nazi feature films for general release. But these films were even more conformist than the official product, because, he asserted, self-censorship was a much stronger force than public laws and policies.

∞

I arrived at Booby's around eleven p. m. prepared for the worst, and I immediately saw it. The pool of possible sex partners was not impressive. In my hometown, the men who stayed behind had aged very quickly after high school and looked older than they actually were. A Midwestern diet and sedentary lifestyle (which was killing my mother) and a tendency to drink too much (which had killed my father) were undoubtedly responsible, and I thought I noticed something else: the hiding required to get by in this town had taken its toll on them. The men looked beaten down and furtive. There was desperation in the air, and I had arrived bringing fresh meat. I needed to have my wits about me, so I ordered a ginger ale. I drank it in silence as my fellow patrons stole glances at me.

As I finished my drink, someone walked in, and the whole mood of the place changed. Everyone at the bar started whispering to each other and pulling disapproving faces. I locked eyes with the man. He was young and handsome, with longish brown hair and a round, almost childlike face that a full beard transformed. His septum was pierced, and I thought about the possibility of other things being pierced. He was much shorter than I, and from across the bar I could see he had an antic way of carrying himself that seemed like an indication of trouble. I happened to be interested in trouble, so I motioned for him to come over and sit next to me. He was happy to see a new face.

"What are you drinking?" I asked.

"Rum and coke," he said, and after I ordered one for both of us, he got directly to the point, "My name is Andrew. I like to get fucked, especially when a tall guy dominates me." He leaned in and asked, "Who are you?"

I told him my name, and since he was being forward, I asked, "Have you ever been fisted?"

"As a matter of fact, I have," he said, and with those words, I kissed him, the kind of kiss that attracted everyone's attention. He caught his breath and said, "Let's go to my place."

"I thought you'd never ask."

As we left, I could have sworn I heard a line from a Marx Brothers movie uttered with a note of huffy propriety, in imitation of Margaret Dumont: "Well, I never!"

I drove us down the main street of the city, under an expressway that divided the "good" part of town from the "bad," and Andrew directed me to park in a small lot next to a large house, the only one on a block that included abandoned industrial buildings, a parking lot full of empty eighteen-wheelers, and a single phone booth stranded at the edge of a field.

Andrew and I climbed the wooden back stairs of the house to his apartment, which, while large, looked barely habitable. The place had clearly been a shoddy addition to the building, with a cramped bathroom and minimal kitchen. Against one wall, there was his bed, a messy pile of mattresses. I took off my jacket and threw Andrew onto the pile. He tore his t-shirt as he struggled to take it off, and I pulled down his pants. He was a hairy little guy and smelled of sweat. He had a "treasure trail" leading from the small of his back to his ass crack. I started eating his ass as he lay on his belly. After a bit, we changed positions, with him sucking my cock while he sat on my face. Then he turned around and sat on my cock, riding me as he looked into my eyes. He said, "Just do me a favor and tell me when you're about to come."

It usually takes a while for me to come when a guy rides my cock, and Andrew's legs were tired of bobbing up and down before I got there. He changed position, I pulled out, and my cock went soft. With him on all fours, I stuck my cock in his mouth, and he sucked it until it got hard again. I got behind him, spat on his ass, then shoved my cock in him again and pumped away. Doggie style had always been my favorite position. As I was about to shoot, I pulled out of his ass. I ejaculated all over the dark brown hair on the small of his back. He wiped the cum away and licked it off his hand. I lay down next to him and whispered in his ear, "Do you have any lube?"

He said, "Yeah, I'll get the Crisco." He went to the kitchen cabinet and came back with a large can. "Sorry I don't have a sling or anything like that."

I said, "No problem, I prefer to fist a guy on all fours anyway."

"Hot."

"Assume the position," I commanded.

"Yes, sir," he said eagerly.

Andrew wasn't exactly the right size to accommodate my hand in his ass easily. Small guys can sometimes take hands, giant toys, even whole arms in their asses, but it takes a lot of work. I kept in mind that Andrew was living in an area where he had few opportunities for practice. I lubed up my fingers and patiently slid them into his ass. He started moaning. I reached his prostate and turned my hand so I could graze it with my knuckles, and he screamed. I backed off, and after he calmed down, he said, "I need to call my landlady next door to tell her I'm not being murdered."

"Am I hurting you?" I asked.

"Hell no," he said. "I'm a screamer."

"Yeah, I can tell." I laughed.

After the call, I started again on Andrew's ass, but no matter how I approached it or what I did to calm him down, I could never get the large knuckle at the base of my thumb all the way inside. This is the most common stopping point for novice fisting bottoms; once they learn to relax and take the widest part of the hand, the rest is relatively easy. Andrew was enjoying himself regardless. At one point, he totally lost the ability to talk and started licking the wall above the bed. I definitely had him where I wanted him.

By the third attempt to get my whole hand inside, I figured I wouldn't be fisting him that night, and I asked, "Have you had enough, boy?"

"Yes, sir. Sorry, sir."

I said, "No need to apologize. I have big hands."

We got up and washed off separately, because there wasn't enough room for both of us in the shower. Before he got in, I told him to kneel down and open his mouth. I pissed, and he drank every drop. "Good boy," I said, and went to the bedroom to get dressed.

I looked around for a wallet. I liked to check the driver's license of a new trick to verify his real name and age. His said, "Andrew Noël Johnson, born April 1, 1968." He was twenty-three years old, his birthday was April Fool's Day, and he was named (intentionally or not) after an impeached US President. Something about that information made me smile.

∞

Once Andrew had dried himself off and put on some clothes, I asked him if he was hungry and if any place around there would be open late. He said, "There's a greasy spoon for truckers. I didn't eat much today, because I wanted to get something big in my ass tonight. I did, and now I'm starving."

We got in the car and I turned on the ignition to warm it up. It must have been below zero outside. The stereo came on, and before I was able to put a cassette in the player, we heard a blast of radio evangelism: "…telling our precious kids the truth and unmasking this vile act for what it is. Anal sex is demonic. There's no other way to understand it. Using the anus as a substitute vagina is a desire from the pit of hell."

I turned down the volume, looked over at Andrew, and asked, "Has potty training become a religion now?" He cracked up, and I reached for a copy of Bob Dylan's *Highway 61 Revisited*. I said, "I hope this is okay with you."

"Definitely," Andrew said, as I turned up the volume to play "Like a Rolling Stone" full blast.

As the song ended, we arrived at our destination, Mom's, an old fashioned diner in the middle of an interchange of highways that defied logic. Overpasses hemmed the place in on three sides, and there was not a single tree or shrub to be seen anywhere in the vicinity. A neon sign was the only colorful element in the sort of drab, monochromatic landscape I saw every winter of my childhood. When we got out of the car, I noticed a tang like rotten eggs in the air. As we entered the place, Andrew said hello to the waitress, and we found a booth as far away as possible from the handful of truckers eating at the counter.

"Come here often?" I asked.

"Only after I get laid, so not often enough."

I said, "Those dudes at Booby's looked pretty rough, and not in a good way."

He said, "Oh, my God, they're just white trash—Mountain Dew drinking, McDonald's loving, fucking yahoos. I mean, I slept with… well, I've had my fair share of those guys. I don't kiss and tell, but this city is getting very, very small." The waitress came by to take our drink orders. I didn't want a Mountain Dew.

I asked Andrew, "What do you do?"

"I work as a caretaker at a halfway house for homeless people. It takes up the rest of that building where I live. And there's a community outreach program where we work with the schools. I run a farming program over the summer with high school kids. I also do courses where we teach people how to use a bank account, work on finances, and show them places to go to get fresh food. The organization does good things, but it's all based around Christianity."

"Like with the Salvation Army, there's a catch," I said.

"Yup."

The waitress came with my iced tea and Andrew's club soda. She took our food orders, breakfast for both of us. As soon as the waitress was out of earshot, I asked, "Have you been fisted lately?"

"The last time I got it regularly was back when I was nineteen. The guy had very small hands and the smallest dick, but he definitely knew how to use them. What I liked about him is that I never really knew what was going to happen. We would get shitfaced drunk and come home from a party, and he would just throw me down and start going at it. Kinda like you did. It was great. He always made sure I was comfortable. We never really had a safe word, but he would pause in the middle and say, 'If you want me to stop, let me know.' It was a very strong trust we had in the bedroom. The whole reason why we met up was for me to be his slave boy. It was really fucking hot."

I asked, "How did things go wrong with him?"

"He would drink a lot at parties. It started getting to be humiliating. He was slapping my face and punching me. I like that occasionally in the bedroom, but not to where it's consistent every time. I would ask him to stop, but he'd be drunk, saying, 'You know you like it.' I'd say, 'No, not right now.' He would say, 'Boy, I have to take a piss.' We'd go to the bathroom and he would piss in my mouth and smack me around a little bit. It was cool, but when he got more drunk, he would continue to do it. He'd get into verbal abuse, calling me nasty things over and over again. I'd be like, 'Dude, this isn't respectful.'"

I told him, "Personally, I don't do verbal abuse. Some people really love it, but I've found it's difficult to manage the boundaries. Once you reach a certain point, you can't take it back and say, 'Oh shit, I didn't mean that.' It's too late."

"Yeah, this guy was very into being the abuser. To a certain extent it was hot, but in the middle of having sex with him the situation could get out of hand. While he was sitting there shoving his feet into my mouth calling me a dirty faggot and saying I'm a worthless sissy, I thought, 'Is he being serious? This is kind of changing the whole atmosphere for me. Is this really all he sees me as?'"

I said, "Sometimes, when you're involved with someone sexually, he becomes an object to you, which is hot, but it's incompatible with companionship, friendship, love, whatever. How do you make those things come together in a way that's reasonable and isn't hurting people? Unfortunately, being reasonable is pretty much impossible when it comes to sex."

He nodded. "I think whenever I start feeling attached to a guy, I have to back out of the situation. I say, 'Okay. I can't do this anymore. This is too much.' I do think deep down inside human beings are not meant to be monogamous. It's a lot of work and a challenge. But I think it definitely has more advantages than disadvantages in the current society we live in."

The food came and we started to eat our eggs. I continued, "When you're having sex, all this stuff plays out inside your head. You get these ideas about the person you're with that may have no relationship to reality. They relate to the porn you've been watching or to your childhood. Who the fuck knows? Your partner, if he conforms to your ideas about what's sexy, can fulfill your fantasy. But the more time you spend with him, the more he becomes a real human being. He may turn out to be a rapist or maybe a Judy Garland fan. Not that those two things can't go together. You know what I mean?"

Andrew's face brightened and he gulped down his food. "It's funny you mention Judy. While I was in that relationship, the guy took me to a friend's house where there was a sex room. As soon as you walked in, you saw floor to ceiling pictures of Judy Garland all over the walls. There was a sling in the middle and this huge stage. It lit up and said 'Boy.' He had one little portable TV."

I asked, "What was on the TV? Was it Judy or porn?"

"It was porn."

"Ah, that makes sense."

There was a lull in the conversation, and Andrew broke the silence by saying, "For fun I do drag. I'm sort of a drag terrorist, I don't even bother to shave off my beard. I look like I crawled out of a dumpster. My drag name is Allison Chainz. Nobody gets it in this town, but fuck 'em." I smiled and let him continue, "There was a whole period when I was reading everything I could about Valerie Solanas, you know, the woman who shot Andy Warhol." I nodded and thought of Amok Books. I wondered how this guy would fit in as a Los Angeles hipster. "I wanted to form a punk band called River of Snot, like in the SCUM Manifesto: a man is so obsessed with sex that he'll swim through a river of snot if he thinks there'll be a friendly pussy waiting for him." I laughed uproariously. "Valerie wrote a play called *Up Your Ass*, and I thought it would be great to do my own version, *Up My Ass*… you know, for obvious reasons. But I never found a copy of it. Has it been published?"

"I don't think so. I guess her family or whoever didn't want any more publicity. Maybe the manuscript has been lost." I looked at Andrew intently for a moment and asked, "Have you gone to college?"

He answered, "No, it's way too expensive for me, even the state schools. I'm on my own." He said in a lower tone of voice, "And I'm crazy. I guess that's one reason why I was obsessed with Valerie for a while. I admired her ability to survive as a mentally ill person. She got a chance to go to college, but nowadays, the crazies who do well are all rich kids with concerned parents and fancy psychiatrists. They go to the best schools and get the best meds." Our happy mood had dissipated. There was a look of bitterness on his face.

The check arrived and I paid it. I said, "It must be difficult for you to get decent medical care around here. Where do you go?"

He responded, "I haven't been able to find a shrink I can afford. There's no clap clinic either, so for that stuff, I go to Planned Parenthood and deal with the protesters outside. I want to say, 'Hey, I'm here for an HIV test,' but that doesn't mean anything to them except, you know, sodomy." We both laughed. "There's one doctor in town at the hospital's infectious disease department, but his wait list is insane. There's maybe ten or twenty doctors in a bigger city, but I can't go that far away. I'm not driving these days. I've had a couple of drunk driving convictions."

"Sorry to hear that. Not much you can walk to in this town. It's bleak."

He sighed and said, "The population is declining fast. I don't want to be here anymore. I'm working for that community outreach program, but it's all religion-based. Like a lot of people, they want to stay in their religious bubble, and nobody else wants to be a part of it. I've got to get out of the bubble, if you know what I mean."

"Hail Satan."

"Hail Satan, sir."

FOURTEEN

When I returned home from the Midwest, I fully understood the consequences of my argument with Daniel. Now there was a void in my life. For lack of anything better to do, I went back to the manuscript that had caused the rift between us, and I started to revise and expand it. I changed Daniel's name to David and John's to Joe, among other things. I continued to write about Raúl, about the clubs and bars of Los Angeles, and about what had led me to move to California in the first place. As the text grew, I noticed that a whole pile of legal pads full of writing had accumulated on my desk. From time to time, I went to the copy store down the street and rented time on a computer to type my work into a word processing program, since I had no computer or printer of my own. I backed up my files on a floppy disk, and I printed out the manuscript every time I changed it significantly. Soon stacks of paper threatened to engulf my apartment. On one of my many trips to the recycling bin to dispose of old drafts, I finally admitted the obvious: I had a book on my hands. The task of writing became so engrossing that I did little else with my free time. Reading no longer occupied my empty hours; the books I picked up didn't appeal to me very much. I was writing the book I wanted to read.

∞

A couple of months after my return, Raúl called me to let me know that he was spending spring break in Los Angeles. The weather in Chicago was too punishing for him, and he needed to get away. I met him the next day at the Thai restaurant that had been our regular spot for a meal after a fisting session.

Early in the conversation, I asked what I most wanted to know, "The last time you were here, we met but you didn't want to play. Was something wrong?"

He said, "Ah, I wondered when you'd ask. No, nothing was wrong. I still think you're sexy and love what we did together…"

"But now you have a boyfriend."

"Exactly," he said.

"I wish you had told me. What is he like?" I asked.

"He's a white guy, a bit older, basically a bear. And he's totally in love with me."

I asked, "Does he live in Chicago?"

"He's in Carbondale. He teaches at Southern Illinois University. So I've been putting a lot of miles on my truck these days."

There was a pause, then I asked the inevitable question, "Does he fist you?" I wanted to know if fist fucking and a serious relationship were compatible for him.

"No, he's not into kink at all. We have married people sex." There was a note of disappointment in his voice, but I was discreet enough not to point that out.

"I see. Are you monogamous?"

He said, "Yes, until further notice. I'm not like Daniel in that way."

"Speaking of Daniel, I'm not playing with him anymore."

"What happened?"

"Oh, we had an argument. You see, I've started to write about my fisting experiences, and I made the mistake of showing an early version of my manuscript to Daniel. He freaked out. He thought I was endangering his relationship with John."

Raúl looked a bit surprised and said, "Well, he can't stop you from writing."

I laughed. "He certainly tried. He gave me an ultimatum. I said I didn't want to be forced to choose between him and my work."

"I told you he was crazy, but you had to figure that out for yourself.... So, am I in this piece of writing?"

I blushed and said, "Yeah, I was going to tell you about that."

"I have no problem with it. Really, I'd be honored. Just change my name, okay?"

"Of course. Do you have a name you prefer?"

"Mario. That was my uncle's name."

I said, "Sounds good. Thanks for being understanding." We ate our food quietly for a little while, and Raúl was kind enough not to ask me a lot of questions about the manuscript, which I was not comfortable showing to anyone. I asked him, "Do you have any plans for your spring break, other than trying to see your father between his trips to the bathhouse?"

Raúl smiled. "I'm spending a lot of time with my mother these days. She's been lonely. But I want to go to LACMA. I've never been there, and a free day is coming up this week. Do you want to go with me?"

"I'd love to."

∞

Raúl and I arrived at the Los Angeles County Museum of Art at about three in the afternoon, and it was already crowded, with more people sure to come after work. The courtyard was swarming with tourists and a jazz band was setting up to entertain them. The County Museum, so big and ungainly, its group of buildings a funny mish-mash of architectural styles, was unfashionable but serious. Something interesting was always on display, though it might take some effort to find the exhibition. At that time, the Getty Center had been getting all the media attention, much of it unflattering, because a couple of years before, the Getty had begun construction on its new site—Moira called it the CIA of art history—a huge complex on a hill above the 405 freeway, a project that would eventually use more stone than the Great Pyramid of Giza. In this context, LACMA, centrally located and easily accessible by public transportation, would forever look virtuous by comparison.

Raúl and I first went to the Japanese Pavilion, a remarkable late building by architect Bruce Goff. Its atmosphere was a welcome change from the chaos of the courtyard. Neither of us had a special connection to Japanese art, but we lingered in the building's tranquil, dimly lit interior. I suggested we might find some quiet in the Prints and Drawings Department, so we braved the crowds and went to the main building. Much to our relief, we were almost alone in the gallery, where we saw an exhibition of recent acquisitions.

We took our time with the prints, looking at them one by one and moving counter-clockwise around the gallery. When we reached the last wall, I discovered the James Ensor print *Doctrinal Nourishment*, the one I had loved when I was in high school. Raúl laughed at the sight of the figures shitting from a great height while the masses below gobbled up their turds. I said, "There's a whole story behind this print."

"I'm sure," Raúl said. "I want to hear it."

"James Ensor, who was an anarchist when young, made this print in 1889, a wretched year in Belgian history, when the religious right dominated parliamentary politics and effectively shut out the left. That meant there were no checks on the power of the central figure in the print, King Leopold II. When he took the throne, he seemed like a dimwit, but beneath his awkward exterior, he was cunning and vicious. Leopold claimed the Congo for Belgium, not as a colony, but as his own personal property, a place outside the rule of law. He got away with this by pretending to be doing charitable works and spreading Christianity among the Africans. What he really did was to set up a system of forced labor to exploit the Congo's vast resources, especially rubber, a commodity in which he virtually cornered the world market at the moment when automobiles were first being manufactured. The Congolese were treated with absolute brutality. Multitudes of men were worked to death, families were held hostage, and children were mutilated if their fathers didn't supply their quota of raw rubber to the Belgian bosses."

"I know what you're talking about. Amazonian Peru had a rubber boom, too," Raúl said, "but go on."

"Eventually, an international outcry against these abuses caused such embarrassment that the system was modified, though it was still colonial. Leopold II surrendered his huge private domain—a place he had never once visited, because he was afraid of germs—to the Belgian state, but only after he had enriched himself enormously. He was possibly the world's first billionaire. The results of this accumulation clutter the landscape of Belgium to this day: monstrously tasteless buildings and monuments that all date from the end of the nineteenth century and the beginning of the twentieth. When I was in Europe a few years ago, I saw some of them, including the Royal Museum of Central Africa, a giant apology for colonialism out in the suburbs of Brussels. The museum doesn't officially acknowledge the other result of this accumulation of wealth, the deaths of ten million people."

I had been concentrating so intently on what I was saying that I didn't notice someone coming up behind me. "Did I miss the lecture?" he asked. I turned around and saw Daniel. Without a thought, I grabbed him and kissed him on the mouth. He said,

"Hello to you, too."

Someone else wanted to take a close look at the Ensor print, so the three of us sat on a bench in the center of the gallery. I asked Daniel, "How have you been?"

"A little tighter than I'd like, if you know what I mean."

"Let's get together soon," I said.

"Please."

Raúl said, "I want to see the rest of the museum," and so we went to visit the other galleries.

∞

On the way home I told Raúl, "Thanks for arranging that."

"I'm happy to do it. You were both being stubborn."

I said, "I wasn't going to bring up the issue if he didn't."

"And thank God he didn't mention it. You two belong together."

"Well, he has that boyfriend," I reminded Raúl.

"Sure, but you're the one who'll help him find himself."

FIFTEEN

After our reconciliation, I went back to work on Daniel's hole with renewed vigor. He had seen other partners, a circle of older men who fisted him, but none of them got the same access I enjoyed, because he trusted me more. I was the only one who could go deep enough to put most of a forearm inside him. Over the course of our meetings, I had almost reached the elbow, and I looked forward to making it there, a project that could take months of sessions. A major appeal of fisting for me was that there is always a new goal to achieve. Regular fucking and sucking paled by comparison.

We tried the "E Ticket" again, and I made tiny increments of progress towards our goal. I noticed that Daniel was more open than usual, and that he could easily take my hand very deep in his ass with no complaints. I turned a deaf ear to Daniel's protests anyway, because they were never very serious. For him "no" usually meant "yes," or at most "slow down." At one point, my right fist entered Daniel's rectum, and I managed to bring in my left hand to cover the fist with it. While both hands were inside, I moved them deeper, until I had a few inches of both forearms buried in his ass. Daniel let out a scream. After I pulled out, I said what I had done, something that always pleased him, because when he took a fist on all fours, he could never see what I was up to. He was especially happy this time. As we lay in bed coming down from the session, Daniel said, "I love you." I remained impassive. I liked it when Daniel sought my approval, and I preferred not to appear vulnerable in his eyes. But I would tell him I loved him one day.

∞

Daniel told me that getting fisted had been bringing back childhood memories, and that he was gaining insights to which he had never had access in any other way. I asked him what he had remembered recently, and he told me a story.

"When I was a child, my grandma would go to an outdoor market to sell things to support us. She would take me to the market with her. It was just the two of us, because there was no one to watch me. She couldn't leave the booth or people would steal things. One time when I was four, I went to the bathroom on my own. There was a man in a stall who called me over to him. He offered me a coin. He started to undress me, but I told him to hang on, and I started undressing myself. He penetrated me, but I don't remember pain. I just remember telling him to stop because I had to potty. At least I thought I did. I have a feeling I knew what he was doing, and it was a normal thing for me. Why didn't I fight against what was happening?"

I asked, "Did someone have sex with you before that?"

He exhaled sharply. "My biological father. At least that's a theory I have. Or it could have been my uncles. Why didn't I question the stranger in the stall? I don't know anything for a fact, but someone was abusing me. I think it was my father because of how he rejected me afterward. He said I wasn't his child. He wanted to distance himself from me because of his guilt."

I asked, "Did you ever seek out sexual experiences as a child, or did you just passively accept what was done to you?"

He said, "I wasn't aware of anything. I wish I could remember more. I would bet money that I was being passed around like a plaything between the men in the neighborhood, my uncles and their friends."

∞

There was a death in Daniel's family, and he had to cancel our next date. He called me that evening and said, "I saw my biological father and half brothers today. My grandma died. It was her funeral."

I said, "I'm sorry."

He said, "She was my father's mother, and I wasn't close to her. I went with my sister. An aunt came up with two guys and told me, 'These are your brothers.' It was a shock. I never saw them before. One of them is gay. They have full heads of hair. You know, that shit makes me mad. Why did I go bald? The sperm donor paced around a lot. He didn't say a word to us. Kept his distance. I could tell he was conflicted."

"I bet."

Daniel growled, "He's not a human being. He abandoned us when we were little. This was his only chance to reach out, and he fucked it up."

I asked, "Did he abandon his second family?"

"No. That family is together. I'm so happy he walked out on us, because he's an asshole. If he hadn't, I'd probably be living in East LA as a wetback. Totally *chunti*, ugh."

"*Chunti*?" I asked.

"You know, an ignorant guy who does the yard work, dresses like a cowboy, speaks no English…"

"Sounds insulting."

"Oh, it is." For a moment, I thought about José from Michoacán and how much fun I'd had with him. Daniel would have called him *chunti*, too. He continued, "I heard the sperm donor had a hard time dealing with his other gay son. If that had been me, I probably would have been a runaway. Thank you, Satan, for letting me be who I am today."

I said, "He must be an ignorant man."

"Yes, and ugly as fuck. I pray I don't look like him when I'm old."

I asked, "Does he look like an ancient Olmec head?"

Daniel said, "More like Leatherface from *Texas Chainsaw Massacre*," and then he hung up.

∞

A couple of weeks after Daniel told me he loved me, he called to invite me to the house he had bought with his boyfriend. John would be out of town on business that week.

I made my way to Sylmar using a combination of buses that took about two hours. I arrived at a single-story ranch style house decorated with New England clapboard. As soon as I entered, I heard the barking of small dogs. The three of them, all from the same litter and nearly identical, rushed towards me and jumped up to the level of my knees. One of them wore an eye patch. I asked what was wrong.

"Oh, Baby lost an eye. The problem with the breed is that their eye sockets aren't big enough for their eyes. If they get too excited, their eyes can pop out." As Daniel said this, he gathered the dogs and put them in their cages. I hoped my visit hadn't excited them too much. I didn't want a dog's blindness on my conscience.

Daniel led me to the guest bedroom. (The master bedroom he shared with John was off limits.) He had placed an array of lubricants, sex toys, and poppers on the table next to the bed. He undressed, got on all fours, and took a big hit of poppers while I greased up my hand.

Progress was slower than it had been in weeks. Daniel's ass seemed tense. I asked him what was wrong, and he said, "Whenever I get fucked at home, I have this feeling my mom is going to come in and interrupt. Let me go smoke some pot. Maybe that will help me relax."

While I was alone in the room, I looked at a bookshelf that contained the couple's entire library: self-help books for Daniel and cookbooks for John. There was nothing that the publishing industry would consider literature in their collection. I felt like a snob judging him and his boyfriend harshly for their lack of serious books. I kept these thoughts to myself. Although Daniel was a smart guy, he never got much of an education—thank you, State of California—and he was sensitive about it. Daniel wasn't a great reader, but he had an extraordinarily vivid inner life. His inspiration didn't come from books, but from what had happened to him in reality.

Daniel came back smelling like skunk, and I made another attempt to fist him. This time, my hand went in more easily. I reached halfway up my forearm, not as far as usual. Daniel said, "Wait!" and I went no further. I didn't move my hand at all while Daniel caught his breath. After he took a hit of poppers, I started to remove my hand, and I decided to do it as slowly as possible. One by one, each ring of muscles in Daniel's colon caressed my knuckles. The move made Daniel react more strongly than I'd seen in a long time. It had never occurred to me before to do something so simple. Over the next hour, I repeated the very slow outward movement, every time with a similar effect. Daniel was screaming. At the end of the session, sweaty and in tears, he said, "That was beautiful." I was pleased that it had gone so well. Then Daniel broke the mood by asking, "Is it okay if I jerk off?"

I was annoyed and said, "If you must," as I went out the door. I decided to take a shower while Daniel masturbated. I thought I had given him orgasms already, and I didn't see the need for him to ejaculate.

After Daniel was done, he took a shower and dressed in the master bedroom while I made myself comfortable on a huge suede couch in the living room. I lay there half-dressed reading the book I had taken on my bus trip, Denis Diderot's *The Nun*. Daniel came out and announced, "I'm hungry. Let's go eat."

Daniel took me around the neighborhood in his pickup truck. There wasn't much to see other than apartment buildings and single family houses. He turned to me and said, "When you refused to be in the same room with me jerking off, it was humiliating. I loved it." He got a faraway look in his eye. In a daze he drove to a sushi restaurant. As we sat in a booth, he told me that this was his favorite place to eat in the area, and he proceeded to order half the items on the menu.

Daniel called himself a pig, and as we ate, I could see that he wasn't referring only to his behavior in the bedroom. He consumed things with great abandon, picking up sushi with this hands when it fell from his chopsticks, spilling rice on the table, eating huge bites at once. He was enjoying himself, but I was a little embarrassed. Daniel noticed and said, "Sorry. When John cooks, he loves to watch me eat. He gets off on it. I guess you're more interested in the hole at the other end." He laughed, and I joined him.

I told Daniel that I needed to get back to my place, and he wasn't bothered to hear it. I didn't feel like spending the night with him. He paid the check then drove me home, about a half hour south on I-5. I was very relieved that I didn't have to deal with the bus system again. On the freeway, he played a cassette of music I didn't recognize, slow dirge-like Goth songs. I didn't particularly like them, but I didn't complain. Daniel said, "John never lets me play my music at home, unless it's dance music."

I remembered the cult of Madonna, and I imagined what petty torments Daniel must have endured while living with his boyfriend.

I got the impression that the relationship had imposed a lot of restrictions on Daniel. He was definitely a freak, but he was never allowed to realize his full potential because of the disapproval of people around him—boyfriend, family, classmates. These people had been holding Daniel back. He came up with interesting ideas, but he had little latitude to express them, except when he was with a sex partner. Perhaps I was the only person who truly knew him. From time to time, Daniel would hint that he might be interested in leaving John, but I never chose to continue that conversation.

When he dropped me off, Daniel said, "Every time I see you, you modify my body. My insides have been rearranged. It's what I've always wanted."

We kissed, and I said, "Thanks for the ride home."

"No, thank *you*."

∞

I knew that Daniel's birthday was coming up, and I bought him a present, a copy of Joel-Peter Witkin's book *Gods of Earth and Heaven*. After a particularly intense fisting session at my place, one during which I very nearly reached my elbow, I told him to clean up really well, because I wanted to give him something. He took a shower and dried off, then I gave him his present. As we lounged on the bed propped up with pillows, he unwrapped it.

Daniel looked through the book, and his eyes welled up with tears. I thought it was because he was touched by my gift, but as he turned the pages it became obvious that he was truly disturbed by the photographs of dismembered bodies, deformed people, animals, and skeletons. I felt a bit of regret that I had given it to him. Trying to save the situation, I asked, "Remember these pictures from the day we met?"

"Of course I do, you loon!" He put the book down and sobbed. I put my arm around him and asked him what was wrong. "You didn't know," was all he could say. After a couple of minutes, he stopped crying and calmed down. He finally said, "I grew up around death."

"During the civil war in El Salvador?" I asked.

"Yeah, the worst thing was the murder of my three cousins."

I gasped. "I didn't know. I'm sorry. What happened?"

Daniel took a long breath. "At the time, Guatemala was helping the Salvadoran guerrillas, so anyone with a Guatemalan accent was immediately suspected of being a spy against the government. El Salvador's government had death squads that would go from town to town killing anyone who might be a guerrilla. They would rape and kill for fun. All of this was funded by the Reagan administration.

"We lived in a small secluded neighborhood. My family was mostly women, and the neighbors didn't get along with them. You know, Third World turf wars and whatnot. My aunt had three small daughters who had lived in Guatemala for a couple of years, and being young they had picked up the accent. They were eight, ten, and thirteen years old. That same aunt had a son who might have been involved with the guerrillas, but he denies it. Who knows?

"Anyway, one night, we were all sleeping and the death squad came to our door looking for the Guatemalans living there—the girls. Some neighbors had informed on them. Their mom was living in the US and hoped to bring them over. My mom was in the US too with the same plans, so we were all taken care of by our two aunts and my grandma.

"I was asleep. They broke down the door and said they wanted the Guatemalans. My grandma tried to explain they were not Guatemalan, they only lived there a couple of years. The death squad claimed they were taking them for questioning, but everyone knew what that meant. They went to take me away, but my grandma threw herself on top of me and they couldn't get her off. So they gave up and only took the girls.

"The girls were butchered. They were raped, tortured, and mutilated. One had her head placed inside her stomach."

I looked down and said, "Like the photographs in the book."

"Remember when I had to turn away from one of the pictures in the exhibition? I was thinking about my cousins. I still can't believe it happened. I just don't understand. My cousins were babies. How could they be spies?"

Daniel continued, "I remember the next morning. We lived at the end of a cul-de-sac at the foot of a cliff, and there were houses above us. A relative lived there, and they sent us children up the cliff to avoid all the adults crying and mourning. I remember looking down from the cliff to our house and seeing the women in the yard wailing and shuffling around in the dirt, like in a trance."

I was totally speechless. I put my arm around Daniel. I held him for a long time in silence. I thought about the landscape he sometimes visualized while I was fisting him, beautiful green hills, peaceful and desolate, seen from a cliff. It was an idealized version of a view he had seen in his childhood, a place he associated with trauma. He was trying to erase that trauma by substituting a pleasant sight for a horrifying one. Getting fisted enabled him to make that substitution, and to understand why he was doing it. I suddenly felt very close to Daniel. I kissed his temple and said, "I love you."

∞

What Daniel had told me about himself was so far beyond what I knew from my own life that I struggled to make sense of it. He sought out extreme experiences that took him to the mental space of past episodes, but he had found a way to relive them on his own terms, under controlled circumstances, with a partner he trusted. He was probably unaware of what he was doing at first, but it eventually became clear that his childhood had made him into the pervert he was. I made my best attempt to understand Daniel, but he still remained an enigma to me in some ways. That was one reason I kept coming back to him. I was indispensable to his project of self-discovery, and that project had no definite end. It reminded me of something Fred Halsted had said, "I put him through a revelation to himself."

I felt real affection for Daniel, and what we shared had brought about a transformation in me. His appreciation for my talents was the strongest approval I had ever received from anyone. I couldn't live without Daniel, but I couldn't live with him, either. He had made a commitment to John. This man understood Daniel's desires, knew that he couldn't fulfill them, and at the same time didn't wish to leave him. Daniel and John had developed a web of obligations that bound them together. Daniel and I had no such obligations to each other. I couldn't provide Daniel with a house, a swimming pool, and three little dogs; I had no interest in living in the San Fernando Valley and paying a mortgage. As far as I was concerned, the situation was fine as it stood. We saw each other regularly to enact our private rituals, but we couldn't be domestic partners, to use the parlance of the day. I had to admit that I felt little desire to live with anyone. I lived my life exactly as I wished to, alone but at the same time not alone.

∞

Later that spring, I made another visit to Daniel's house in the Valley while John was out of town. Daniel promised he would be more relaxed, and that he'd keep the dogs under control this time. I reluctantly made my way to his place on the bus. I was in luck—the transfer didn't take very long, and I arrived in an hour and a half. Since I was a bit early, he wasn't quite ready for me yet. He showed me a new item of furniture, an expensive massage chair, and said he'd be done when my massage was finished. I sat in the chair, but once I was alone, I got up and looked around for something to read. On a table in the room I noticed a stack of papers that looked familiar. It was my writing. The pages were a bit stained. A long time had passed since I'd sent the manuscript to him, and I guessed that he left it in plain sight on purpose.

Daniel came into the room, and I said, "I see you still have my manuscript."

He smiled. "Yeah, I couldn't send it to the landfill. I threw it away, but then I got it out of the garbage can when John wasn't looking."

"Are you okay with it, as long as I change your names?"

He walked over to me and looked me in the eye. "There's nothing in it that could ruin my relationship. Besides, I trust you. I know you'd never hurt me. So, yeah, everything's fine. And I love the writing."

I said, "Good, let's play."